COMING HOME TO YOU

OLIVER & DEMI-LYN

THE KERRIGAN FAMILY
BOOK 2

ANDREA FINNELLY

CONTENTS

PROLOGUE

Oliver Kerrigan stood at the edge of the lake near the resort his parents operated. They owned it with their siblings after being passed down to them by his paternal grandparents, but his parents were solely responsible for managing it. His uncles had wanted other careers, yet they all still had a hand in making sure the resort had what it needed to be the best place to stay in town.

He liked that his family had this history in Cypress Bay. Their resort was a big part of why tourists came to town. An hour away from Orlando, most tourists bypassed them for the theme parks. But for those looking to get away from the crowds and overpriced vacations, this was where they came.

Cypress Bay Manor Resort—Cypress Manor as his parents called it—was on Lake Tola, which gave them a ton of water activities to take part in every summer with their friends and family.

The private beach was for guests only, but seeing as they owned the resort, his friends and family used it all the time. They had a dock with a gazebo at the end that his grandfather had built for his grandmother. He fished off that gazebo many times with his brother, Simon, cousins, Luke and Noah, and their friends, Sean and Joel. Their cousin, Ryleigh, always wanted to tag along and fish, too, but they didn't want a girl hanging out with them.

Joel had a secondhand boat, and he would take them out onto the lake in it. It wasn't a big boat—just enough room to fit two or three of them at a time. He had become a good boat captain, and Oliver wouldn't be surprised if Joel eventually took off on a larger ship someday. Taking the boat out further into the lake meant they frequently caught bigger fish without having to throw them back into the water. Oliver often took them to cook over a campfire for his family and friends for weekend dinners.

He loved to cook and couldn't wait to leave for culinary school in a few weeks. It was his passion, and he itched to be in his own kitchen someday—preferably the one at Cypress Manor.

After looking out over the lake and beach, Oliver gazed over at his family and friends. His brother Simon and his friend Joel weren't with them again this year. They were two years older than him, and they'd both left for a quick backpacking trip before heading back to college. They would usually come home for a month during the summer break, then leave for whatever activity or place they wanted to explore before the new school year started.

His cousins, Luke and Noah, were identical twins, but they couldn't be more different in their personalities. Noah was the oldest by a few minutes. He was getting ready to finish his bachelor's degree, then he'd head to medical school to become a doctor. He finished his associate's degree while he was still in high school. Oliver admitted Noah was the smartest of them.

Luke was all muscle. He was the "bad boy" of the family, always getting in trouble. Never enough to be hauled off by the sheriff—he wasn't that sort of "bad boy"—but he definitely had a reputation as the troublemaker of the bunch. Luke worked out all the time and had more muscles than anyone else at his age, but no one would ever mess with him or anyone else he cared about; that was for sure. College was out, much to the dismay of Uncle Lou and Aunt Amanda. Instead, Luke planned to join the Army and was set to leave in another two weeks.

Oliver smirked as Luke, Noah, and their friend Sean tried to build a huge monstrosity of a sand castle on the beach, while their younger cousin, Ryleigh, tried to build a moat around it. Their other cousins, Katia and Marinda, were trying to convince them to decorate the castle with shells, but the guys weren't having any of it.

Ryleigh, Katia, and Marinda were their fifteen-year-old— going on sixteen—triplet cousins. Officially, they were a pain in his ass that wouldn't go away. Unofficially, they all worried about the girls. Especially now that they were getting older and catching the attention of all the boys. With all the guys leaving, it would mean the girls were on their own. Sure, his parents, uncles, and aunts would keep an eye on them, but it wasn't the same thing.

Their father—his Uncle Riley—was doing his best to raise them on his own. They were all aware that their mother abandoning them at a young age left a mark. The adults tried to keep what happened from the older cousins, but it didn't take much to figure it all out over the years.

Hailee rounded out the cousins at almost seventeen. She wasn't related by blood, since his Uncle Joshua and Aunt Felicia had adopted her as a baby, but she was theirs. No matter how much she tried to keep herself apart from them all.

Right now she was reading by the pool near her parents, sitting under a huge umbrella. She always said that with her light complexion and auburn-red hair, she didn't want to burn playing on the beach and would rather sit under the umbrella next to the pool. They all understood it was another way for her to keep to herself, so everyone always made a point of spending some time with her when they were all together. At that moment, Sean's sister, Emma, and another girl who visited every summer were trying to coax her out to help with the castle.

The other girl was becoming a problem in his mind. Demi-Lyn Shaw and her family had been coming to Cypress Bay Manor Resort every summer to stay in one of the new cabins by the lake. Her parents liked the area so much that they recently bought a small vacation home on the lake and planned to retire in Cypress Bay.

Demi-Lyn met the triplets playing around the lake, and she immediately clicked with Katia, who became her summer best friend. Her parents also became friends with his parents, uncles, and aunts over the years. They were always invited to spend time at the private beach with them even though they had their own lake access next to their vacation home.

Oliver shouldn't be thinking about Demi-Lyn at all. He was almost eighteen and about to go off to culinary school. Demi-Lyn was only fourteen. Besides, she didn't live in Cypress Bay. Her family lived somewhere in Maryland. By the time he finished school and lived his life a little, she would be all grown up and heading to college herself. Chances were their paths wouldn't cross again anytime soon unless she visited with her parents. Even then, he'd most likely be spending most of his time in the kitchen at the resort.

He knew Demi-Lyn had a crush on him. If only she hadn't started changing from a gangly little girl who followed them all around into a pretty teenager, who was still way too young for him. He especially loved her long, curly brown hair. It was so long he often wondered if she got tangled up in it when she slept.

The thought of how stunning she would be when she was

older made him shiver before he reminded himself of how old she was now.

Clearing those thoughts out of his mind, he headed over to his father and uncles, who were building up a campfire on one side of the private beach. They purposely made it small for Oliver to grill up some of the fresh fish they caught earlier for dinner.

His father, John, and Uncle Lou were building the fire, placing stones around the edge and twigs in the center, while Uncle Joshua and Uncle Riley stacked up some larger logs nearby. They planned to expand the fire into a larger one after they ate. The whole family and their friends would sit around the fire talking for half the night. Sometimes guests at the resort would stroll by and join in. It was always something Oliver looked forward to, and it was something he would miss when he left.

Walking up to his father and uncles, Oliver stopped to help. "Hey, Dad."

"Oliver! Just the boy I wanted to see," his father boomed.

Oliver rolled his eyes. His father was always calling him a boy when he wanted him to start seeing him as a man. His father didn't mean anything bad by it and was mostly teasing him. But he was almost eighteen, damn it! "What can I help with, Dad?"

"Go up to the resort and grab the fish we caught and prepped, will ya? We left it in the cooler in the kitchen. There should be a cart you can use."

"Sure thing," Oliver replied, turning toward the resort.

"And bring the vegetables in the containers next to the fish. Take someone with you to help," his Uncle Lou suggested.

"I'll help!" Demi-Lyn rushed up to where he was walking.

Oliver didn't want any help, especially if it was from her. "You don't need to come, Demi. There'll be a cart to carry it all," he said, still walking toward the resort. Maybe if he walked fast enough, she would become discouraged and go back.

"Sure, there's a cart, but that doesn't mean you won't need help. What if something falls off when you're pushing it? I can grab it to make sure it doesn't fall onto the ground."

He was practically jogging to the resort now, but he forgot that Demi-Lyn enjoyed running and was on her track team in Maryland. Bloody hell!

Knowing she wasn't going anywhere, and that he didn't want to overheat before having to cook over the fire, Oliver slowed down and came back to a walk.

No point in trying to get rid of her; she wasn't going anywhere.

Besides, her family was leaving tomorrow morning, and then he would leave in a couple of weeks. He reminded himself that this would most likely be the last time he'd be around her.

Oliver could handle one more night.

Walking around to the back of the resort to the delivery entrance, Oliver held the door open for Demi-Lyn and followed her through into the kitchen. The kitchen was absolute mayhem with people working at every surface, preparing food for the dinner rush. The head chef was yelling at his station chefs to move the food along or to cook it to perfection, while the kitchen porter was running around taking orders to complete multiple tasks, like grating some cheese and cleaning up a spill.

He loved every moment.

This was his environment. A place where the chaos in his head disappeared as he immersed himself in the chaos in the kitchen.

Oliver started working in the resort kitchen as soon as he was old enough to legally work. He began by helping in the dining room, Tola Dining. It wasn't what he wanted to do and was pissed off about it at first, but over time he understood why his parents told him he had to start at the bottom.

His plan was to go to culinary school and eventually take over as the head chef at the resort. If he wanted to be worthy of that job, then he needed to work in every part of the business. Lately, he had been helping as a junior chef, helping the station chefs and learning everything about the kitchen process.

Besides the dining room, his parents added a British-style tavern, BritSip, as his mother was missing a part of her heritage. His father thought the tavern would fit in with the resort. He wasn't allowed to work in the tavern yet since he wasn't eighteen. But he spoke with the manager of BritSip all the time to glean how they operated with the kitchen.

And they were just starting the plans to add a poolside eatery that his mother wanted to call The Basin. That would serve all-American type fare, like burgers, hot dogs, fries, and ice cream. He'd miss the opening, but it couldn't be helped.

Ignoring everything going on around them, Oliver directed Demi-Lyn over to the full walk-in cooler away from where everyone was working.

"Can you grab the cart around the corner?" Oliver asked as he opened the cooler and walked in.

"Sure, be right back."

Looking around the cooler, he found the fish laid out in a large container of ice. Bins of cut vegetables were stacked with the shucked corn next to them, ready to grill over the open flame.

"Here you go," Demi-Lyn said as she pushed the cart into the cooler.

Picking up the larger container of fish first, Oliver set it on top of the cart. Demi-Lyn started grabbing the vegetable bins and placed them on the bottom of the cart. When they were all done, Oliver wheeled the cart out the cooler door, making sure it was closed behind them.

Several times on their way back to the beach, some of the vegetable bins shifted off the cart because of the rough path. He wouldn't tell her, but inside he'd admit he was glad for her help.

Back at the beach, Demi-Lyn went back to her family, while Oliver started seasoning the fish and vegetables, placing them on the makeshift grill over the fire. This was where he was in his element. His chest swelled with pride at being able to cook food for his family and friends. Watching them enjoy what he made was even better.

Later that night, after everyone ate, they settled around the larger fire and relaxed together. Oliver would really miss this. It wouldn't be forever, he reminded himself, but he would be so far away from home. For the first time, he was leaving Florida to go to school in New York City's much colder climate.

He couldn't wait to experience everything there was to learn about the culinary arts. The sooner he went, the sooner he'd come home. The head chef already said he was planning on retiring in another five years. Plenty of time for him to earn the job...gain the experience he needed, maybe work in a few other restaurants, then come up with some new ideas to bring back with him.

Feeling a little melancholy—and if anyone ever said he was, he'd deny it—Oliver stood from his camp chair around the fire, said goodnight to everyone, and walked toward the resort to head to his car.

His family used to live at the resort in a private apartment on the first floor, but as he and Simon got older, his parents wanted a separate home for them. They currently used the apartment now when his grandparents came to visit from England, or for close family friends.

Oliver knew that at some point Simon would live at Cypress Manor since he was preparing to take over the resort someday. He was okay with that. He didn't want all the headaches of running the entire resort and would rather be in the kitchen. And he would never want to live at the resort where he'd be bothered at all hours.

His dream was of a home on the lake, away from the hustle of work, to relax and create in a kitchen of his own.

The night had a pleasant breeze—if a bit warm—his body a little overheated from the fire and night air. Instead of walking straight to his car, Oliver strolled down the beach a little toward the trees to take the longer path through the woods back to the parking lot. The temperature dropped a little as he entered the green space, cooling him off.

Hearing footsteps behind him, he turned. A figure was running toward him at a fast clip; her long legs ate up the space between them.

"Demi, what are you doing here? You should be with your family."

She stopped right in front of him, practically toe-to-toe. Not wanting to show how much his body reacted to her, he stood his ground, crossing his arms. In reality, he knew she only had to look down, or take a step closer for their bodies to touch, to find out how he really felt about her.

"We're about to go back to the lake house, and I wanted to say goodbye since we'll be leaving to go back home tomorrow morning."

"I already said goodbye when I left the beach."

"That was just a general goodbye to everyone. I didn't want to miss saying good luck with school. You're going to be a great chef, Oli."

He wouldn't admit how much the nickname meant coming from her. She was too young for him. And they were both leaving soon.

"Thanks, Demi. Have a safe trip home," he said, turning to continue walking away, dismissing her.

"Wait!" she exclaimed.

As he turned, Demi-Lyn wrapped her arms around his neck, pressing her mouth to his in an unpracticed and innocent kiss. Oliver's hands unconsciously went to her waist to hold her steady.

Before he registered what was happening, the kiss quickly ended. Demi-Lyn unwrapped herself from him and ran through the woods toward the beach and her family without looking back.

1

Twelve years later.

Demi-Lyn Shaw drove down I-4, monitoring her GPS for the exit to the road leading to Cypress Bay. The setting sun gave the sky a glowing darkness with just enough light to see the road ahead, her own headlights on so others would view her in the dimming brightness.

She'd been to her parents' vacation lake home many times growing up as a kid, but she had never driven to the place as an adult. Once she graduated high school, Demi went off to college on a track scholarship and stayed at school with her friends, working and hanging out over the summer breaks.

She was nervous about coming back to Cypress Bay. Not because she was worried about seeing her childhood summer friends again. She kept in touch with Katia Kerrigan, and she kept Demi updated on what everyone was doing, telling her she wished for her to visit again.

But over the years, she knew she couldn't come back. It was too painful for her to see Oliver and not remember how she felt about him. Just thinking about him made her heart pound and her skin flush.

Her parents thought it was a young girl's crush. It was not. She loved everything about him.

But things changed.

Painful events made her really look at her life and decide Cypress Bay was where she needed to be, even if Oliver was never in her life. Maybe they'd be friends. She would need to be okay with that. Because this time she wasn't coming for a summer vacation—never mind that it was January, so obviously not. No, now she was coming to make it her permanent home.

Thinking back, Demi reflected on what had changed. Her parents' death was the catalyst for all her rash decisions. She realized she wasn't handling it well. Had it been seven months already? It all seemed to merge in her mind.

She was finishing up her shift at the office when a pair of officers came to her workplace. That was when she found out her parents had been killed in a freak car accident. She still didn't understand what really happened to them. The officers said it was a single-car accident and that somehow they believed a faulty part caught fire after the car hit the tree, causing the whole car to burst into flames. Her parents were trapped in their car, or knocked unconscious from the crash; the officers weren't clear. Whatever the reason, they couldn't exit the vehicle before the flames overtook them.

Demi still didn't understand. They were on a remote road with no one else around. It wasn't raining—it was a bright sunny day. Her father was a good and careful driver. He would do nothing to put him or his wife at risk. Her parents adored each other. The officers said they suspected an animal crossed their path, causing the accident. She wasn't sure whether she believed them.

They wouldn't even look into the accident anymore,

deciding it was a simple one-car accident with no crime to investigate. Again, Demi wasn't so sure about that.

She wanted to believe it was nothing more than an accident, but she really couldn't work it out in her head.

Her parents had been the best a girl ever had.

Her father, Marc Shaw, was a tall Caucasian man at six-three. It was the only reason Demi grew to a respectable five-seven and had curly hair, while her Filipino mother, Malaya Shaw, was a paltry five-zero with hair as straight as a pin.

Their love story was one they told Demi frequently growing up. He was stationed in the Philippines way before the United States pulled out of the bases in the 90s, but that wasn't when her parents met. Instead, they met when her father went to Manila to visit friends and her mother was hanging out with her friends. They all ended up at the same nightclub, where her father and his friends had reserved a table. Her mother and her friends had nowhere to sit, and when Marc spied Malaya across the room, he quickly offered them a place to sit at their table.

The rest worked itself out, as her father always said. Her mother told Demi he refused to leave the country until she agreed to marry him. Her father laughed and said he didn't go that far that fast. Then they'd give each other a look that made Demi want to leave the room.

Just thinking about them together made her smile until Demi thought of how she would never see them again. This thought led her back to thinking about the crash. She wasn't able to identify her parents. With nothing left of them to identify, Demi had no reason to even look, the officers told her.

Amazingly, the only thing to survive the crash and fire was her mother's rosary beads. Her mother wasn't a devout Catholic—Demi snorted at the thought—but she always carried a string of rosary beads in her pocket that had been passed down from her grandmother. Somehow, it was the only thing recovered from the accident still in one piece. Demi carried it with her everywhere she went ever since she collected it from the officers who informed her of their deaths.

It wasn't the only thing Demi had of theirs, though. They had a house in Maryland. Marc and Malaya Shaw were not pack rats at all, but their office was crammed full of books, notes, and computer equipment. She packed all of it up to look through later. Demi was sure some of the financial papers would be important, though she didn't have time to look through everything yet.

Demi's car was on its way out, so she sold it. Instead, she packed it all—the office boxes, a chest of keepsakes her mother kept in their bedroom, scrapbooks, photo albums, and anything else she deemed irreplaceable—into her father's old Jeep Cherokee that he kept in the garage for when he went fishing and a 5x8 cargo trailer.

Now, an estate company was going through what was left. They'd sell what they could, and clean out what they couldn't before the real estate agent put her parents' house up for sale.

Demi quit her job last week, so that wasn't an issue any longer, but she would need to find a new one soon. The money she had in her own savings was minimal, and until the house sold, it was all she had to live on. Thank goodness she had her parent's lake house in Cypress Bay. Otherwise, Demi didn't know where she'd be living.

"In one mile, turn right." The sound of the GPS talking snapped Demi out of her pensive thoughts. Concentrating on her location, she flicked on the turn signal and veered into the exit lane.

Now that she was on the road heading toward the lake home, she recognized local landmarks. The nature park gate on the left was locked up tight for the night. She always liked to hike the hilly paths, though it was usually uncomfortably hot in the summer.

A couple of stores and businesses had changed hands in the years she had been away, but the buildings were still the same.

Turning onto a less densely populated road, Demi was getting eager to arrive at the home and settle in for the night. It had been a long couple of days driving down, and that was after all the weeks of sleepless nights trying to deal with what was left of her parents after working full days.

As Demi was about to reach the turnoff for her new home, she heard a crack and pop before losing control of the Jeep. Fighting with the steering wheel, Demi moved it and the trailer to the side of the road. Not seeing the ditch in the dark, the vehicle tilted to a stop partway in the ditch.

Damn! Now what was she going to do?

It was possible to walk to the lake home, but she didn't want to leave all her stuff sitting on the side of the road. Looking around, there was not a single light or building visible—just trees.

Katia was aware she was coming tonight. But what would she do? *OK, Demi...you can work this out yourself. No problem.*

Before she exited the Jeep, headlights appeared from around the corner. Thank goodness, she thought, hoping they'd stop to help.

2

After a long day at work, all Oliver wanted to do was grab a beer and a nice meal, sit on his couch and catch a game on tv—he didn't care which one—a long hot shower, and a good night's sleep. In that order.

He loved his job, but some days it was more about getting people to do what he wanted them to do, or stepping in between arguing employees, rather than actually cooking.

That was what he got for wanting to become the head chef, he supposed, though he was more like the executive chef. He understood what he was getting into as far as becoming the head chef was concerned. Not that he did not know, but as an executive chef he was in charge of more than just the food.

For once, he would like to do more than wrangle people—those in the kitchen and those working the dining room. Oliver wished he had realized that his job would be more like being the CEO of the kitchen and restaurants. He was in charge of the kitchen, Tola Dining, BritSip Tavern, The Basin, all their employees, inventory, and any other supplies needed.

It was exhausting.

Oliver admitted it wasn't like he was running all over the

place all day. If he had to be everywhere at once, he could never go home. He employed people under him who helped manage each area. He had a couple of sous chefs in the kitchen, who overlapped in some duties with him and each other. One had the morning shift and the other the night shift. Plus a team lead for the dining room.

He had a manager in charge of the tavern. She was responsible for hiring and managing the bartenders and for making sure they were well stocked. Since any food ordered from the tavern menu came from the main kitchen, that was one area she didn't need to worry about.

The Basin got its food inventory from the main kitchen's food storage—ventilated pantry, walk-in refrigerator, and walk-in freezer—before they opened each afternoon. But they prepared everything to order at the poolside eatery. Because it was smaller than Tola Dining, the manager was also one of the cooks. He was more like a team lead, with minimal responsibility, other than making sure he had enough food for the day and managing the few employees who worked at The Basin.

Every week, Oliver would meet with the sous chefs, tavern manager, and both the dining room and eatery team leads. Then he would take their reports and create his own—he hated reports—before having another meeting with his brother, Simon.

Thankfully, there were no meetings today. He actually loved days when he immersed himself in the kitchen, getting to create meals for the resort guests. He loved it even more when he had time to experiment with new recipes and menu ideas. Oliver realized he hadn't given himself the time to do that recently. He would need to make some time this weekend, if possible.

To be honest, he was having problems concentrating on anything these days. He realized it was because he still hadn't allowed himself to move past the anger stage in his grief, even though it had been a year since his mother's death. Okay...he knew she was never coming back, but he was just so angry that his mother wasn't with them anymore and the man who hit her got off with barely a scratch.

The man was in prison, sentenced for life because apparently he was a habitual drunk driver, and actually killing someone was too much this time. Oliver was still angry that they did nothing about the guy after one of the many other times they arrested him for drunk driving. If they had, his mother would still be with them today.

One thing he was happy about was not having to corral his father anymore. John Kerrigan lost the love of his life and went into a tailspin trying to distract himself from how much pain he was experiencing. He'd been causing all kinds of problems at the resort, which he had retired from to spend more time with his wife traveling. When she was killed, he didn't know what to do with himself anymore and came back to the resort, insinuating himself into their employees' jobs and making a right mess of everything.

Thankfully, he pulled out of it about the same time his brother needed someone to set him straight so he wouldn't lose the love of his life. Simon was now happily engaged to Aylin, and they were planning their wedding, while their father now worked filling in where needed at the resort.

He was short a server, though. He had one leave last year, then today the server who replaced her didn't show up for her shift. Again. He and the team lead had to scramble to find someone to take her place for the day. This was the third time she either called in or didn't show up for work. He would need to let her go and find someone else to replace her. But first, he would need to find the time.

Maybe he'd let Simon find someone. Oliver hated the entire

hiring process. Besides, his brother was the CEO of the resort, not him.

Thank goodness this workday was over. He was almost home and looking forward to that beer and meal. As he turned the corner, a vehicle with a cargo trailer was parked on the side of the road...no, it was tilted in a ditch, its hazard lights flashing brightly in the dark. Great, just what he needed. A disabled vehicle, someone needing help, at the end of an already exhausting day.

Pulling over, Oliver couldn't ignore someone in need. Especially out here where there were fewer places to get help. As he pulled over to assist whoever was having problems, a person got out of the vehicle. When the woman was bathed in his headlights, he quickly realized it was Demi-Lyn Shaw and cursed. Of course, it had to be her!

Slowly getting out of his SUV, Oliver took in Demi while he was still in shadow, his body nothing but a black outline from her perspective.

She had definitely grown up from the kid she was the last time he saw her twelve years ago. Demi filled out a great deal. She had way more curves than she had at fourteen. She cut her hair. It was now up to her shoulders; soft curls bounced around them, and she had some sort of sweeping bangs that went to one side. He found himself disappointed that her gorgeous brown-black hair was no longer down to her waist. She was average in height...at least compared to his six foot two.

"Hi, I'm so glad you came by when you did and stopped. I was about to call someone to help."

Oliver was angry that she would jump out of her car like that, not knowing who it was stopping to help her. For all she knew, he was some sort of serial killer or something. What would she have done if he had been someone stopping to hurt her?

"What are you doing getting out of your car? I could be a stranger wanting to hurt you," he growled at her.

Demi froze after hearing his voice. "O-Oliver?"

He walked up to stand next to her, where she would be able to clearly take him in. "Yeah...it's me," he said much softer now. He didn't want her scared of him. He may not be happy she was unexpectedly thrown at him this way, but the last thing he wanted was for her to be frightened.

"What are you doing out here? Not that I'm unhappy to see you. I'm glad you stopped to help me," she added.

"I live out here now. What happened?" The last thing he wanted to tell her was that he practically lived next door to her. She would find out soon enough.

"I don't know. I was driving and heard a pop. I must have run over something. I was able to pull over, but my Jeep got stuck in the ditch."

"Okay. Let's take a look. Got a spare tire?"

"Yes, my father always kept one, but the back is filled with boxes and luggage on top of it."

"All right, let's look at your tires first. We'll only take out the spare if we need it." Crouching down next to the vehicle, Oliver quickly figured out the passenger rear tire had a hole in the side. It would not be an easy fix with where the vehicle was in the ditch.

"How does it look?"

"Well, it will not be easy, but we'll manage. I need to pull my SUV in front of you and hook you up to drag it out of the ditch and onto the street, then we can move some of what's in the back to squeeze the spare tire out."

Oliver walked back to his SUV and pulled it in front of Demi's Jeep Cherokee. He was lucky that she already had a hook on the front. She said this was her father's, but he was having a hard time thinking about her driving a beefed-up SUV like this. It just didn't fit with how he thought of her, especially when he hadn't seen her since she was a kid. He guessed he really didn't know her at all anymore.

Quickly hooking up her vehicle to his, Oliver had her put her car in neutral while he dragged it out of the ditch. It would have been easier if they had unhooked the trailer first, he thought. But he'd still make it work. He just needed to go really slowly, so he wouldn't tip everything over.

Once they had it back up on the street, Oliver unhooked it from his SUV. Together, they unhooked the cargo trailer and started shifting all the boxes and luggage out of the way. Some too big to shift had to be taken out and temporarily placed on the ground.

"I'll take this to get it fixed for you," Oliver said once he had the new tire on. He took the old flat tire and loaded it up in his SUV before she even thought to refuse.

"Oh, um. I could have done that."

"That's okay. You look like you have enough to take care of," he said, pointing to the boxes and luggage on the ground. "You actually shouldn't be towing the trailer with the spare. Why don't I hook it up to my SUV and bring it to the lake house?"

"Ummm...I guess that would be all right."

"Let's load you back up and get on our way."

They quickly put everything back into the Jeep before moving it out of the way, hooking up the trailer to his SUV. Demi told him she was going to park it in the garage for now. He nodded to her before getting back into his vehicle and followed her to the lake house.

He really didn't want her to find out he lived next door yet, but he had no way to keep her from figuring it out. He would just need to tell her. When they got to her house, she opened the garage door, and he backed the trailer into it.

"Thank you for helping me. I couldn't have done it on my own," she said after they'd unhooked the trailer, closing the garage door.

"No problem. That's what friends do, right?" he asked.

"Yeah...something like that. Would you like to come in for some coffee before you go?"

"No, I need to get home," he said.

"That's right. You said you live out here now. Is it close?" she asked.

"Yes, it's close," he said, dreading her reaction when she found out just how close.

"Okay, well. I guess I'll see you later."

"Let me know if you need any more help. I'll get your tire fixed and bring it back to you," he told her.

He got back into his vehicle, started it up, drove out of her driveway, down the street one house, pulling into the driveway on the other side of the house next to hers. Getting out, he looked over at her and shrugged when he saw her standing in her driveway with her mouth dropped open in shock.

"Goodnight, Demi," he called out before walking into his house and closing the door.

3

Seeing Oliver again so soon after arriving in Cypress Bay shocked her. Demi thought she'd have more time, but evidently that wasn't meant to be. The idea of seeing him again sent her body into overdrive.

He grew out of his teenage looks and into something that was harder and more angled. His dark hair was mussed up as though he'd had a hard day and ran his hand through it repeatedly. He now had a short beard and mustache that looked more like perpetual scruff. She wondered if he had always had that or if he just hadn't shaved in a while. His brown eyes made her feel more alive than she had in a long time.

Apparently, she hadn't gotten over him in all the time she'd been away with how her heart raced. She wasn't about to admit that the first thing she wanted to do was jump into his arms. She barely resisted.

Then he surprised her again when he drove out of her driveway. Oliver apparently lived a house over from her! Why did he buy that one? It wasn't a secret that her parents' house was on this side of the lake. Did he buy it on purpose with the hope she'd come back?

Demi scoffed at herself. Of course not. Oliver would never buy a house just because it was practically next door to the house her parents owned. It wasn't like he ever gave her or her parents any sign he was interested in her.

Another thought occurred to her suddenly. Did Mrs. Tepen still live next door? That thought made her shudder. Not that she didn't like the older woman; she was sweet and would always give her a cookie or let her play around her backyard. But Demi remembered that every time they came out of the house, her parents would become entrapped in conversation with her. She was a talkative woman and wouldn't let anyone go anywhere without a full-on conversation. Her parents always said she was lonely, and so if using a little of their time to talk to her made her happy, then that's what they would do.

Demi wasn't sure she was ready for Mrs. Tepen's brand of talking every time she stepped out the door. She would need to reconsider keeping the trailer in the garage and move her car inside instead. Then she'd have a way to skip all the extra conversations when she left the house.

This morning she needed some time to be alone. Demi had a horrible night—between the fright she had on the road, running into Oliver before she was ready, then all the memories that bombarded her when she entered her parent's vacation lake home for the first time in years—she barely got any sleep.

Sleeping in the room she had as a child, she didn't remember the bed being so uncomfortable. And tiny. Demi was used to having a larger bed where she could stretch out. But she wasn't ready to sleep in what had been her parents' bedroom. After tossing and turning last night though, she'd clean up the master bedroom, put on some of her own pillows and sheets to make it hers. She'd sleep more comfortably in the larger bed tonight.

But first, she would empty some of the boxes and luggage

from the Jeep. Last night she grabbed only one suitcase with clothes and toiletries. She needed to bring in the rest of her stuff and make the place start to feel like her own home rather than her parents'.

She'd eventually need to go through her parents' clothes and anything else they left here, but she wasn't sure she was ready for it yet. One step at a time, and the master bedroom was far enough for now.

Fortunately, her parents left little at the lake house because they only came down during the summers. But her mother always said it was easier to have a summer wardrobe that stayed so she didn't need to lug a bunch of clothes back and forth each summer. Plus anything she bought in town ended up remaining in Florida.

Demi's room looked almost exactly as she had left it the last time she came down with them when she was eighteen, before she left for college. She never came back. She wondered if any of the clothes in her old closet still fit and she'd like to keep.

Well, she couldn't figure any of it out if she just stood around letting memories flow through her. Time to go grab some boxes out of her father's Jeep. No...it was now her Jeep. She didn't think she would ever get used to it.

Sadness swept through her at the thought of never seeing her parents again.

Shaking it off, Demi stepped out of the house. As she walked toward the vehicle, Oliver caught her eye standing at the fence separating his property from Mrs. Tepen's. Looked like he got caught by their neighbor and was stuck talking to her. Hoping she'd escape without Mrs. Tepen seeing her, Demi tried to sprint back into the house. Before she made it, the older lady turned her head.

"Oh, Demi-Lyn! I'm so sorry about what happened to your parents," she began as she walked toward her, rather spryly for someone who surely must be a hundred by now. "I was just telling Oliver here when I saw your father's Jeep how surprising it was to hear about them. You must be so devastated!"

"Hi, Mrs. Tepen. How are you?" Demi didn't want to be rude, but she did not want to talk about her parents or anything about how they died.

"Oh, I'm just fine. Bones are aching and my joints hurt, but that's normal for an old woman like myself. I'm more concerned about you, dear. Why don't you come over and have some tea and cookies like you used to? Are you staying here at the house? Or are you getting your folks' place ready to sell?"

Several times, Demi tried to insert a word in, but Mrs. Tepen wasn't having it. She just kept on talking right over her, asking questions yet not giving her the opportunity to answer any of them. This was what made her happy, Demi reminded herself. She's just a lonely woman. Her parents handled it every summer, so she'd do the same. Repeating this inside her head wasn't really helping as much as she'd hoped.

Oliver sidled up next to her, putting his arm around her shoulder and whispered in her ear, "Just keep nodding, she'll eventually wind down."

All she wanted to do was grab some more boxes out of her car. Was that too much to ask? Why did she need to stand here and listen to Mrs. Tepen? And now Oliver was wrapped around her. She didn't have the bandwidth for this right now. It wasn't fair after the rough night she had.

Oliver looked like he'd had a great night of sleep. His hair was styled back, and no longer mussed up, though the top was on the longer side. He still sported the scruffy beard and mustache, so she assumed that was his normal look. He was dressed in another pair of slacks and a polo shirt with the resort logo on it, just like he was last night, she realized. This must be what he normally wore to work, which meant Mrs. Tepen pulled him away when he was trying to leave for work.

"Mrs. Tepen, it was nice talking with you this morning, but I really must get Demi inside. We have a lot to do this morning. She did just arrive late last night." Oliver jumped right into the one-sided conversation when the older woman wound down, made their excuses, and moved them to her front door before Demi realized what was happening.

"Just keep on walking. That's right. No, don't look back at her. It'll only encourage her more," he coaxed as they made their way inside, closing the door.

4

Oliver slept like crap, spending the entire night thinking about Demi-Lyn Shaw. And since he couldn't sleep, Oliver decided he would rise early and take her damaged tire in to the auto shop before heading into work. Instead, he ran into his busy-body neighbor, who wanted to talk about Demi-Lyn moving back and how she remembered her and her parents when they came to visit every summer.

Before he'd been able to extract himself from Mrs. Tepen, Demi came out of her house and got pulled in by her, too. He couldn't leave her standing outside with the woman, all shell-shocked and floundering. The last time Demi was around the older woman, she was just a kid. After all the trouble she had last night, he thought she wouldn't be up for Mrs. Tepen's ramblings. So he stepped in.

But he made a mistake. Putting his arm around her made his breath stutter. And when he whispered in her ear, her scent was like a mixture of some sort of sweet flower and baby powder. Her shiny hair was soft against him as he leaned in, the curls wanting to connect with the scruff on his face and never let go. Her body fit up against his own as if it belonged—as though they were meant to go together like two puzzle pieces.

Now that they were back in her home, he wondered what the hell it was about her that riled him up so much? Why was he even letting her get to him, anyway? He wasn't interested in her. He barely ever thought about that innocent kiss she gave him when they were just kids. Everything was good in his life, so why did she need to move to Cypress Bay permanently?

"What was that?" Demi asked.

"Mrs. Tepen? She's always like that. It's amazing anyone ever has a chance to chime in around her, or even leave for work on time for that matter. I can't tell you how many times I've had to sneak out to my car just to prevent her from catching me on my way to work."

"No, not that. What was up with you snuggling up around me?"

Oliver couldn't figure out whether she was angry or just confused. He would prefer confused. That's how he felt. Anger he could deal with, but that would actually confuse him even more. He did just save her from Mrs. Tepen...so what would she be angry about?

"I don't know what you mean. There was no snuggling up," he said with a sneer. "I was just showing solidarity so Mrs. Tepen's attention wouldn't be all on you. And you have to admit, it worked."

"I guess. Don't do it again." She didn't want him to help her? Fine...the next time Mrs. Tepen waylaid her, he'd leave her to the older woman.

Looking around the room, he noted very little had changed from the last time he was inside. The Shaws tasked his Uncle Lou and Aunt Amanda with managing their property when they were out of town. Since he lived so close, they often asked him to stop by to make sure everything was all right or to drop off some supplies before they came down. Now it looked like a time capsule.

He wondered what it felt like to Demi. He thought she hadn't been back since she had left for college. What was it, probably seven or eight years now?

He bought his place five years ago and took a year fixing it up. She had never come to visit in all the years he'd lived in the home. But maybe she came every once in a while for those first couple of summers between classes. He'd need to ask her to be sure. And obviously, this didn't seem like the right time for that. Anyone except perhaps Mrs. Tepen could see that Demi wasn't ready for twenty questions. Her eyes held a world of pain. Yet she still held her body straight, her head held high.

"Okay." He peeked out the window. The older woman had finally gone back into her own house. "Looks like the coast is clear. I'm going to go. I'll bring your tire back when it's fixed. You may want to move your car into the garage eventually. It's the only way you'll make it out of here without Mrs. Tepen seeing you. Some days I wish my home's garage wasn't converted into another room."

"You don't need to take in my tire. Just leave it here, and I'll take care of it later today."

"Nope. I already called the shop and have it in the back of my SUV."

Oliver walked out of the house before Demi could say anything else. It was rude, but staying any longer was a bad idea. No way was he going to let her take care of the tire. Who did she think he was?

Her father would turn over in his grave if Oliver let Demi take care of the tire on her own. He was the old-fashioned kind. He had always liked the man. They would sit on Oliver's back porch drinking a beer during the hot summer evenings and just talk.

He missed the old guy. The stories he told and the places he went were amazing. Oliver would always tell him he needed to write them down, but Mr. Shaw always said he had plenty of time for that; he would rather live life instead of write about it. Now he was gone, and so were his stories, along with his wife. Two more people gone too soon, just like his mother and paternal grandparents. How much more loss did the universe think he'd be able to handle, anyway?

Snapping out of the melancholy thoughts, Oliver dropped the tire off at the auto shop. After the mechanic, Logan, told him he would fit it in around his schedule for pickup later that afternoon, he drove to work thinking about what was on his schedule that day.

It was a lot of the same—paperwork that he never expected to need to do as a head chef, some meal planning for a new menu he was considering, and if he was lucky, he'd work in the kitchen actually preparing some food—but he had a meeting with Simon scheduled. He wanted to talk to him about hiring a new server for Tola Dining. Maybe he would have better luck finding someone who was reliable and stuck around long enough to make it past the probationary period.

Later that day, Oliver was dead tired as usual. A small kitchen fire was thankfully contained to a pan and rapidly put out by the quick-thinking sous chef. He got the dreaded paperwork out of the way and helped in the kitchen, which always calmed him, even with all the chaos going on around him. He didn't have a chance to look at the menu, but he'd work on it this weekend at home. Though he was thrilled with how his meeting with Simon turned out. Simon probably wasn't happy that he'd dumped another task on him, but he'd get over it. At least he agreed to look for a new server for him.

Now he was on his way to pick up Demi's tire before going home. Oliver wondered what she had been doing today or if she got waylaid by Mrs. Tepen again. She was a pest, but he loved the old woman. She always brought over the best-tasting cookies he had ever had. If all he had to do was sit and talk with her occasionally, he'd gladly do it for those cookies alone.

Not to brag, but he was an excellent cook. Baking, though, was out of his scope. He was rubbish at baking cookies that were crispy around the edges, yet chewy inside. Nor was he able to make pastry flaky without it being too dry. Oliver admitted ages ago that he would never be a pastry chef. Luckily, he'd hired a pastry chef, Daisy Velle, who made amazing desserts for the resort. She was great to work with and planned desserts that complemented his menu.

Pulling into the shop lot, Oliver walked inside and inquired about Demi's tire. He was surprised when the owner, Gabe West, came out to talk to him instead of Logan Barton, who fixed the tire.

"Hey, Oliver, we had a problem with the tire you brought us," he said as he shook Oliver's hand in greeting.

"What kind of problem? Was it too damaged to be fixed?"

"Not exactly. Logan found a bullet in the tire."

Oliver couldn't comprehend what he was hearing. They found a bullet in Demi's tire? How was it possible?

"The damage to the tire was consistent with someone shooting at it," Gabe continued. "So we had to call Luke, and he picked up the tire."

Someone shot at Demi while she was driving. Was it an accident? Oliver mentally slapped himself. Of course, it wasn't an accident. No one shot off a gun in that area. There were too many houses nearby, and while she drove through a largely wooded area, it was part of a state park and hunting wasn't allowed this time of the year.

"Thanks for calling Luke, Gabe. I guess we'll wait to hear what he has to say about it. Do you have a tire in stock that would fit her Jeep Cherokee? It's that old one her father used to drive all the time." He wouldn't even think of her continuing to drive on the spare tire.

Gabe went to check and came back with the tire Demi would need. Oliver paid for it and loaded it up into his SUV. Before heading out, he texted his cousin to find out what he had on the tire he picked up earlier.

His cousin didn't pull any punches with him or any of them for that matter. He was a succinct type of guy and didn't use more words than were necessary. He figured it had something to do with being in the Army, but Luke was like that his entire life.

His attention went back to Demi as he drove out of the parking lot and headed toward home. He wasn't sure what he was hoping would happen with her. He liked her as a kid, but he really didn't know her now that they were adults. She was dealing with a lot, though, and seemed to hold up.

Oliver didn't understand what she went through when her parents died, or how she got through everything in Maryland on her own. Add in someone shooting at her, and he didn't know how she was coping. Though someone could have been randomly shooting and Demi just happened to be in the wrong place at the wrong time. Still, it made his blood boil.

Pulling into Demi's driveway, Oliver took the new tire out of his SUV and leaned it up against the back of her Jeep. He didn't want to disturb whatever she was doing inside, so he also took out his own jack and wrench and began changing her tire.

Actually, he was counting on her being busy. Oliver wanted to go home before she noticed him and what he was doing with her car. When he heard the door open, he knew that would not happen.

"What are you doing?" she called out from the doorway.

"What does it look like I'm doing?" he casually countered while continuing to remove the lug nuts.

She walked over to him and studied the new tire. "This isn't my tire. I was told it couldn't be fixed."

"Right, so I bought you a new one. You can't drive forever on the spare tire." Examining the spare, he added, "It needs to be replaced, too."

"I can buy my own tire," she insisted.

"Of course, you can, but let's just say I'm doing this as a favor for your father, okay?" He looked up at her as he said this. She looked sad at the mention of her father, but she nodded and let him continue changing her tire. Not trusting himself to stay around Demi when she looked like that, Oliver quickly finished up, made his excuses and went back home.

5

Early the next morning, Demi woke up thinking about the previous day. She had packed up her parents' clothes and personal effects at the lake house—with a brief break when Luke came by to tell her the tire had a bullet in it! Her head was spinning with all the thoughts running through it.

Who would want to shoot at her? She told Luke that she didn't really fathom why someone would shoot at her Jeep. She hadn't been to Cypress Bay in years and she didn't have any enemies—unless she counted Elizabeth Masters from middle school. He said it was probably an accident and she just happened to be there. Demi didn't think he really believed that.

To take her mind off that topic, she continued to clean out the house. Her parents had more than she thought they did. Of course, she hadn't been coming down with them for quite a while, so they probably picked up most of it during the years she was away.

She also changed the sheets on her parents' bed. Demi thought sleeping in her parents' bed would be weird. Instead, it brought back nice memories of when she used to crawl in with them at night as a child. She slept better last night than she had in a long time.

Besides cleaning out some of her parents' belongings, she also brought her boxes and luggage from the car into the house. With only a few more small boxes to unpack, she'd leave them for later.

This morning though, Demi was going to empty the trailer. She had no idea where she was going to put everything. She didn't have time to actually go through it all—especially all the boxes from her parents' office. And the last thing she wanted was an enormous pile inside the house within view until her heart was ready to unpack them.

She considered leaving them in the trailer, but she really wanted to move it back outside and park her car in the garage. So for now, she would first move everything out of the trailer and into the house, move the trailer out and the car in, then figure out where to put all the boxes later. Hair up in a ponytail, dressed in sneakers, sweatpants, a tank top and a long-sleeved shirt over it, Demi got to work.

It was hot work with the garage closed up. She was running back-and-forth carting boxes, having shed the long-sleeved shirt ages ago. More than once, she almost opened the garage door to let in whatever cooler air was available outside. It was unseasonably cooler than average for this time of year in Florida, yet she would welcome it at that moment just to give herself a break from the heat she created from working.

Then she thought about running into Mrs. Tepen again and changed her mind. Much better to be a little hot and sweaty now than to spend most of the day fending her off, while trying to unload all this, too.

Katia Kerrigan, Demi's best friend, came to visit her later in the afternoon at the lake house. She had other friends up in Maryland growing up, but none as close as Katia.

It had been too long since they'd seen each other. While

they continued talking throughout the years she was away on the phone or by text, there was nothing like having her friend with her in person. Katia was exactly who she needed to remind her to stop working and take a lunch break.

"Wow! That's a lot of boxes!" Katia said when she stepped inside the house.

"I know, and I still have more," Demi said, letting out a huge breath as she looked over at them.

Demi wasn't even done pulling them all out of the trailer yet, and they were already stacked high against the living room wall. How so much stuff could fit into the trailer was a mystery. She didn't think she'd kept much from her parents, but it was hard to let it all go, so she packed most of it up to look through later. She actually had more from her parents than from her own apartment.

"Where are you going to put it all when you're done?"

"I've been thinking about that. Some I'll go through right away and can unpack, but the rest will need to go up into the attic for a while. I'm just not ready to go through all of them yet." Demi had marked each box well, so she had a general idea of what was in each one, or at the very least which room it came from in her parents' Maryland home. She tried to put them together when she took them out of the trailer, but it really looked like a jumbled mess right now.

"But never mind all these boxes, let's sit down and have some lunch. I want to hear everything that I've missed down here after all these years," she said, changing the subject.

Thankfully, Katia got the hint that she wasn't ready to talk about her parents anymore. They walked over to the kitchen and sat down in the breakfast nook to eat the sandwiches Katia had brought with her. She caught Demi up on all of her family members, and what was going on in town, even though Katia had been keeping her up to date about them over the years.

She was surprised that Simon was engaged and to a writer.

Demi enjoyed Aylin Miller's books occasionally; some of them were even among her father's books as she boxed them up from his office. She wasn't sure if she was excited to meet her or intimidated.

"What are you going to do after you finish unpacking and moving boxes?" Katia asked once they finished their sandwiches.

"I'm not sure. I left my job, obviously, and I don't really have a plan of what I want to do down here yet. I'm here to stay, and that's all I really know," she said, shrugging a shoulder.

Demi never really liked her job in an office, where she basically pushed papers all day. She'd like to try something that allowed her to walk around more so she wasn't always sitting down.

"Well, why don't you talk to Simon and see if he has anything for you at the resort? You always liked the place, and maybe it would be good for you to be around people who are familiar to you. Simon, Oliver, and Marinda all work there every day, and Ryleigh is at the resort more days than not. Besides, you'll also be closer to downtown and me," she said with a smile.

Demi thought about it for a while and figured it couldn't hurt to call him and follow up with him. He may not even have anything, but if he did, working at the resort would be really nice.

Once Katia left, Demi continued to bring in the rest of the boxes from the trailer, finally emptying it. She would hook it up and drive it around the side of the house to park it later that night after it was clear Mrs. Tepen was asleep. She was uncertain about attempting to ignore her, but she just wasn't ready to listen to stories about her parents yet. Demi would make it up to her another time and invite her over once she got settled in.

Now that it was all in, the pile looked huge to her. Why did she bring down so much? And it still wasn't everything. Demi still had some boxes left in the Jeep, but those could wait since they were mostly full of stuff she packed up from her apartment.

Some boxes contained photos. When she was ready, she would take some time going through the albums. Demi also had some boxes marked *Office*. She wasn't sure exactly what they contained. She did a quick look through one box and spotted some paperwork and a few journal-like notebooks. Paging through one of them revealed some weird information that didn't seem to make sense. Maybe this belonged to one of their clients? She would need to have more of a mindset to go through all the papers and journals later. If anything belonged to one of her parent's clients, then she would need to figure that out and return it to them.

She should start putting some of this up in the attic. Nodding to herself, Demi walked to the hallway and lowered the stairs going up to the attic.

She had only been in the attic a few times when she was a kid, usually following her father when her mother wanted something they stored for the winter while they were away. Her mother would always tell her she didn't like to have stuff out when they were away from the house for a long time. So she would pack up some of it at the end of every vacation and have her father lug it up the stairs to store.

Climbing the stairs, Demi pulled on the string hanging from the ceiling, bathing the room in soft light. Stepping onto the plywood floor, she ducked around the joists crisscrossed under the roofline. The space wasn't large, but it took up the entire length of the one-story, two-bedroom house. Looking around, it was clear her mother definitely had her father drag a bunch of stuff up.

That thought had her sinking to the floor. It would have been a week before they died. Her parents were supposed to stay longer, but something came up and they called her to say they were coming home early. At the time, she didn't give it a second thought.

Demi had her own life, lived in an apartment, and had a decent job. But her parents always communicated when they were going to Florida or coming home to Maryland. Demi just figured they had a new project. It wouldn't have been the first time they'd cut their summer vacation short for a new job. She remembered a few disappointing summers, where she wanted to stay, but her parents said they needed to go home because others counted on them.

Her father was an accountant, her mother was a bookkeeper, and they worked with a lot of different companies. They started the business when she was eight, the year before they started coming down to Cypress Bay for summer vacations. As she got older, she found out they contracted with many people in high places around Maryland, Washington, D.C., and Virginia. To her, they were only her parents. Wonderful and yet flawed at the same time.

She soon realized that, for an accountant, her father was better with money when working for others than he was for himself. Oh...they had enough to pay their bills, take summer vacations, and live well. But they really had little saved. It was all tied up in their homes and a couple of retirement accounts. Once she paid off their debts, there would be little left in their checking account, while the savings account was not any better. The sale of the house in Maryland would provide the bulk of her inheritance. The agent said she already had some interest, so hopefully it would not be too long of a wait. Without a job, the money would be welcome.

Though she'd rather have her parents back than any money their deaths provided.

With that thought, Demi let the rest wait. Instead, she'd call Simon to inquire about a job. Maybe keeping herself busy and out of the house would help keep the desire to escape at bay.

6

Oliver finally had a day where he could work in the kitchen doing what he did best—cooking. He enjoyed the rest of his job, but he wanted to be a chef, not a paper-pusher like his brother, Simon.

Finishing up a plate and passing it over to the server to take out to the customer, Oliver signaled to one of his sous chefs to take over the station. He wanted to check over the dining room and make sure everything was moving smoothly. Being down one server, the others were trying to fill in—though it wasn't always easy during their busier times. He wondered whether Simon had interviewed anyone yet. Oliver would need to stop by his office later and ask where he was in the process. They needed that new employee months ago, even before he let the last one go, if he was honest about it.

Stepping out into the dining room, he immediately witnessed Demi sitting down with Simon and wondered what she was doing talking with him. Why would she come over to the resort to visit Simon? He thought she was at home cleaning up and moving in. Oliver narrowed his eyes at them until he reminded himself how devoted Simon was to Aylin. If she was going to come to his restaurant at the resort, why didn't she ask for him?

Oliver walked over to them, eyeing Demi suspiciously. Why was she here?

"What's going on?" he asked, his arms crossed as he glared at Simon and Demi.

"Not that it's any of your business, but I'm talking to Simon about a job. Got a problem with that?"

A job! She wanted to work at the resort? Why would she want to go and do that? Wait! Did that mean Simon was interviewing her for the server position? No, Oliver didn't want her to invade his workspace. He already had a hard enough time with her practically living next door.

"You want to work here, in my dining room?"

"We haven't decided where she might want to work. That's what we were just talking about. I have several positions available to be filled. Yours is just one of them. Since you're here, why don't you tell her about what is required for the server position?" Simon asked, looking at him with amusement.

His brother was trying to rile him up. He didn't have time to interview for his own position, and yet here he was taking time out of his day basically doing it anyway. Reluctantly, Oliver told Demi what would be required to work at Tola Dining, what hours he was trying to fill, and what the pay for the position was. They paid more than usual for servers because they didn't allow tips. It was all part of the resort experience for their guests and encouraged more locals to come in and dine at the resort. The other downtown restaurants around them were stiff competition, so they had to be just as competitive.

When Oliver was done, Simon told Demi about the other positions available at the resort.

"Why don't we go speak to some people who run the other

departments before we decide which is the best fit," Simon said, standing from the table.

"Good idea," Demi agreed, standing with him.

Oliver was tense; an uneasy shiver flowed through him as they walked out of the dining room together. What would he do if Demi took the job at his restaurant? Oliver thought about it for a while and couldn't think of why she would want to take the server position. Last he heard, she was working in an office up in Maryland. She would probably take one of the other jobs at the resort. Or better yet, maybe he'd suggest a job at one of the new office buildings on the outskirts of town. Surely, she would like that better than working here.

The last thing he wanted was to work with her all day, then have her around again in their neighborhood, too. He would call Simon later and make some alternate suggestions. Maybe Demi would feel better working in one of the offices with his brother or behind the front desk.

Relieved with the decision, Oliver continued going over the dining room to make sure it was running well despite the missing server. They were fine. He didn't need to hire anyone right now. They'd manage a while longer until someone else came along for the job. Satisfied with that train of thought, Oliver went back into the kitchen to work on the new menu he was thinking about trying.

Philip Heaton was not a patient man, nor was he very forgiving when things didn't go as planned. And right now he was furious at the two men he'd hired to take care of the woman and retrieve what was his. It had been months, and still nothing.

That they took care of the couple rather quickly and efficiently was the only thing keeping the men alive. He needed them to finish the plan, retrieve what belonged to him, and take care of the woman. After that, well, he couldn't have too many people around him who knew the truth.

To those who worked for him, he was the consummate businessman. His company was aboveboard in all ways, at least on the surface and as far as legalities played into it. If it weren't for the Shaws, he wouldn't need to concern himself with retrieving information that no one else should know about, nor would he need to involve others with the information that would be costly for him.

But he had no choice. The items were not with the couple, nor were they in their home. It took a while for them to check it out. By then, their daughter must have come by and packed it all up. The men he hired had been following her for a while now with no sign of where she put her parents' boxes. Until they caught her hooking up the trailer and driving out of town.

Philip found out about the Shaw's place in Florida before he hired them. He knew every detail of the lives of those he employed.

The man slammed his fist down on his desk hard, right before the knock on the door, his receptionist peeking inside.

"Mr. Heaton, there's a call for you on line 2. Um, is everything all right, sir?" the woman hesitantly asked.

"Yes, that will be all," he replied, expecting her to leave and close the door immediately.

Picking up the phone receiver, he punched line 2. "This is Mr. Heaton, how can I help you?" he said, putting on his best business persona.

"Boss, we have a problem."

Philip Heaton growled into the phone. "How many times have I told you not to call me on my business line?"

"Sorry, Boss," the man muttered.

"What's the problem?" he asked, more disgruntled by the incompetence of the men he hired.

"We shot at the woman, forcing her to pull over, but before we could get to her, someone showed up to help her."

The man continued to tell him what happened, not leaving out any details. Those he employed for more dubious tasks understood to keep nothing from him. Doing so would mean trouble, in the form of losing limbs or worse, his life.

After the Shaw's daughter left Maryland, he had the men drive straight to Cypress Bay, giving them explicit instructions to take care of her quickly with as few eyewitnesses as possible.

And they messed up everything!

By the time the man finished, Mr. Heaton was incensed. "Continue to follow her. If you have the opportunity, grab what belongs to me. We can take care of her later if need be. I can't afford to have her still walking around. But find what's mine first!"

Slamming down the phone, he was tempted to smash it like he usually did to the burner phones he kept in his desk drawer. But that wouldn't stop their incompetence or prevent anyone from knowing about the call.

They'd better find what belonged to him or it would be the end of them. He'd make sure of it.

The men followed the woman when she left the lake house, keeping a respectable distance so she wouldn't realize they were behind her. She pulled into the employee parking area of the Cypress Bay Manor Resort. Finding a spot to park, they watched the woman as she exited her Jeep and walked into the building.

"Now's our chance to check out the boxes she has in her car," one man said. With the area more crowded than around the home, they needed to be careful not to be seen.

Waiting until no one was around, the men got out of the car

and confidently walked toward her vehicle. Taking a quick look around to make sure no one was watching, the other man smashed the window with the tire iron he held in his gloved hands.

"There's nothing here but clothes and junk."

"Fuck! What about those boxes shoved behind the passenger seat?"

The men continued to ransack the boxes, not finding what they were looking for.

Angry they still couldn't complete their mission, the men pulled out knives and sliced her tires, hacking away at each one before noticing people coming toward them in the parking lot.

"Come on, let's get out of here before someone sees us."

Ducking behind some of the other cars, they quickly worked their way back to their car, driving off while planning their next move.

7

After saying goodbye to Simon, Demi practically skipped as she walked through the parking lot. Glad she had come to the resort, she was thinking about the job possibilities and going through the pros and cons of each one in her head. There were some good options available.

The first option had her working in the offices with Simon. She was highly qualified, but did she want to continue working in an office setting pushing papers? It would be a good job. Little interaction with the guests...that was a plus sometimes. But she would also be stuck in an office all day, where she'd be bored and lonely.

The second option had her working at the front desk under Marinda. She liked Marinda, so that was a plus, but she wasn't sure she wanted to have so much face-to-face time with the guests, who often went to the front desk with problems at the resort. She would be the first person they'd come to when they were angry with something. On the other hand, she would also have the opportunity to help people who were happy to see her. Unlike with the office job, she wouldn't be sitting all day, but standing in one central location for the duration of her shift. It would be something she would need to consider as a possibility.

And finally, the last option had her working for Oliver in the dining room as one of the servers. Could she work for Oliver? Would her feelings about him impact her work? How would he feel about her working for him? All those unanswered questions aside, the job overall kind of ticked all the boxes. It allowed her to work with the guests and not be stuck in an office all day, but the guests were relaxed, eating and talking, making plans for the day, or recounting the adventures they'd taken. The food was superb—what she had while sitting with Simon was wonderful—so hopefully that meant the guests rarely complained about their meals.

She'd be on her feet all day, though she wouldn't be stuck in one place. Demi would walk and move around more during every shift. It was as far removed as possible from what she did before, and for some reason that made it more appealing to her. She would definitely need to think about what it would mean to work for Oliver and to have him live one house over, too.

Demi was so lost in thought that she didn't realize what was in front of her until she walked right up to her Jeep. The side window was smashed, the back door open, all the boxes she had inside were trashed lying around on the ground, and it looked like her tires were slashed, too. Damn it! Oliver just replaced one of those!

Demi scanned the surrounding area. She felt uncomfortable, as if she was being watched, but no one appeared to be around her. The parking lot was empty, but the thought that whoever did this was still around made her uneasy.

Turning toward the resort, Simon was thankfully still outside speaking with one of his employees, his back turned to her. Demi started running toward him.

"Simon! Simon!" Her breath hitched, panic beginning to build as she moved closer and closer to him.

Simon turned around, took one look at her, and ran toward her. "What happened? What's wrong?" he asked as he reached her, holding her up as she slumped against him.

"S-someone broke into my car," she stuttered out. She felt numb. Who would do this? First someone shot her tire; now someone broke into her car and vandalized it. Why was this happening?

"Demi, take a deep breath. Relax, we don't want you to hyperventilate. That's good. Take another one," he coached until her breathing evened out. "Good. Now...someone broke into your car?" he asked.

She took another deep breath. "Yes, the boxes I had in it are scattered around the ground. The side window is broken, and the back door is open. And someone slashed the tires, too."

"Okay. Stay right here while I check it out," he told her. Demi nodded to him, wrapping her arms around herself as he walked away.

Simon carefully walked around her car, noting all the damage, before pulling out his phone and holding it up to his ear to have a conversation with whoever he called. Demi couldn't make out what he was saying from where she was standing, but he looked to be growling at the person on the other end. Most likely, he was telling the person what had happened. He was angry, though she didn't know if that was because of what happened to her, that it happened on his property, or due to whatever the person on the other side of the phone call was telling him. Whatever it was, Simon was pissed.

She only hoped he wasn't mad at her for bringing whatever this was to his resort. Demi was already feeling shaky over the break-in. She didn't want to add guilt on top of it.

Putting away his phone, Simon took another look at her car before walking back over to her. "It looks pretty bad, but it can be fixed. I called Luke, and he'll be here soon. Do you remember Luke?"

"Yes, I remember him. Besides, he came by the other day when they found the bullet in my tire."

"What! What bullet? When did this happen?" Simon looked as though he didn't like being kept out of the loop. It wasn't as though anyone was keeping this from him on purpose. She hadn't even told Katia when she came to visit, and she was her best friend down here.

Demi told him what happened the other night when she first arrived in Cypress Bay, including how Oliver came to her rescue, brought her tire in, and came back to change it with a new tire for her when it was found the old one couldn't be repaired.

"It seemed to be an accident. No reason to make a big deal out of it," she told him. He shouldn't be mad at Oliver or Luke for not telling him either, since it occurred near her home, not the resort.

Well, until today. Now it was Simon's business.

Luke drove up and got out of his patrol car. "So I hear you're causing more trouble, Demi-Lyn," he said with a smirk, walking up to them. Luke was one of the few who still called her by her full name and could get away with it.

She sighed, knowing he was trying to make light of the situation to help her through what was happening. She appreciated it while being upset he wasn't being serious at the same time.

Luke was as much a big brother to her as the others in the Kerrigan family—other than Oliver. They always looked out for her and the girls every summer. She was a little envious of the triplets and Hailee because they got the boys every day of the year, while she only visited them during the summer months. Katia confessed one time that while it was sometimes nice, it was also a pain always having them around, especially once the girls started dating. Demi still would have loved to have them around, but she didn't disagree with her friend about their interfering with their dates.

"Luke, I'm sorry you need to keep on coming out for me." She didn't come down to become a burden to the Kerrigan family. She just wanted somewhere she felt safe and loved now that her parents were gone. It looked as though that would not happen now.

Luke took two large strides, stopping right in front of her. He was more serious now than she had seen him in a while. Not that she'd seen him recently. The boy she once knew was gone, and a man with some serious muscles was in his place.

"Listen, you will not think that way, got it? You will never be a burden to us," Luke said sternly.

Simon shook his head at her and walked away, raising his phone once again to his ear.

"Now let me investigate, then you can give me your statement, okay?" Demi nodded her head and figured it was best to keep her mouth shut for now, letting Luke do his job.

He walked around her car, taking out a small notebook and writing something inside. Every once in a while he would direct someone with him to take some pictures. When they were done, Luke talked to a couple of his deputies, and they pulled out some yellow tape and began cordoning off the area around her car.

A few others began milling about—mostly guests staying at the resort who were curious about what was going on.

When Luke came back to her, she went over everything that had happened, including how she thought she was being watched when she first walked up to her car.

"We're going to need to keep your vehicle here while we investigate further. Do you need anything from it for the night?"

"No, I have everything I need for now," she said, eyeing all of her boxes strewn around the car.

"Don't worry, we'll clean everything up when we're done, and I'll make sure someone brings it all back to you. Your Jeep will need to be towed so that the tires and window can be fixed. I'll call Gabe's shop and have them come pick it up."

How was she going to manage getting back to the lake house? And what was she going to do once she arrived home? Was she safe in Cypress Bay? Would it have been better if she had just stayed in Maryland?

Questions kept swirling around in her head, one after another, to the point where she just wanted to sit down or hide under her covers in bed until it was all over.

"Don't worry, Demi-Lyn. We've got you. As long as I'm around as the sheriff, you'll be safe. I promise." The stare he gave her more than promised her safety. She didn't remember him being so intense when he was younger, but as long as she wasn't the bad guy, it made her feel safe.

She almost felt sorry for whoever was doing this—almost.

8

Damn this paperwork!

Sitting at his desk in the small office off the kitchen, Oliver went over the last of the inventory and manager reports coming in from the various restaurants at the resort. It was the last thing he wanted to do and the last thing he had to do before he left for the day.

He worked through most of the day without thinking about Demi...okay, he mostly wasn't thinking about her. But now that he had to do this paperwork, his mind kept veering back to her. Would she take a job at the resort? And if she did, would it be with him?

He was equally excited and afraid of the prospect. Oliver admitted that her showing up—not just at the resort but in Cypress Bay—did interesting things to him inside. He thought his reaction to that kiss when they were kids was because she had caught him by surprise.

Now he wasn't so sure.

But he also wasn't sure he wanted her near him all the time. She was already living near him; could he resist if she was also working with him? He was afraid he would do something if she were too close to him. When he saved her from Mrs. Tepen and put his arm around her, whispering in her ear, the only thing he thought of was nuzzling her neck. He was too close to doing it and had to stop himself before he did.

His cell phone ringing redirected his attention from Demi and his paperwork. Noticing it was Simon, Oliver got a weird sensation in his gut and hoped it didn't have to do with Demi and a job.

"What's up, Simon?"

"There's been an incident out in the parking lot, and I need you to come out here."

An incident in the parking lot. What the hell? Why would Simon need his help with it? "What do you need me for? I'm sure you can take care of whatever little fender bender took place in the parking lot. I'm trying to finish up those damn reports you need."

"Oliver, it's Demi," Simon whispered.

"Demi? What happened? Is she hurt?" Forgetting all about the paperwork, Oliver jumped out of his chair, ready to run out of his office. Was she hit by a car? The thought of her hurt had him ready to go after the person who did it.

"No, she's not hurt, but someone vandalized her Jeep. She won't be able to drive it. Can you take her home? Don't worry about the reports for now. You can do them tomorrow," Simon added.

Oliver agreed and told him he would be out in a minute. Now that he knew she was unhurt, he relaxed. Taking his time closing everything up, he shut down his computer and grabbed his keys before leaving his office.

What kind of vandalism would prevent her from driving the Jeep home? Did someone shoot at her tires again? That was pretty dramatic already. Who shoots at a moving car?

Oliver was concerned about what this meant for everyone. Cypress Bay was a pretty safe and small tourist lake town.

There wasn't much crime here. Of course, a stalker came after Aylin last year. But that was specific to her. The person responsible had followed her down to Cypress Bay from Philadelphia and then recruited another person to hurt Aylin. Thankfully, Luke prevented the stalker from killing Aylin like she wanted to, and Simon got his happily ever after in the end.

But now they were talking about Demi. He didn't like the idea of someone intentionally going after her. Was it someone who didn't want her coming back to Cypress Bay to stay? Oliver couldn't think of anyone who would want to do anything bad to her.

Simon told him that her Jeep had been vandalized, but he didn't go into any details. Maybe Oliver was making it a bigger deal than it really was. For all he knew, her car had been keyed or something, though that wouldn't explain why she would need a ride home. He would just need to check it out for himself. He walked through the kitchen, down the hall, and into the lobby before stepping outside.

A couple of sheriff's office vehicles were sitting with their lights on in the parking lot. Walking a little quicker, he sensed he would not like what happened to Demi's Jeep. Coming closer, Oliver got a look at it. The actuality was far worse that what he initially imagined.

Then got a look at Demi. She was with Luke while he took her statement, and she seemed to be shocked by what happened. Oliver went over to talk to Simon since Demi was busy with Luke.

"I thought you meant that someone spray-painted or keyed it or something. It takes some real anger to do that much damage," he said with a growl, looking at the damage done to and around her Jeep.

"You would know all about that, huh?" Simon taunted.

Oliver was about to lose his shit with his brother. Everyone knew he kept a lot of his emotions inside, but once they built up too much, it turned to anger. His temper had gotten the best of him occasionally growing up. He had controlled it more as an adult, but what he was seeing now wasn't helping.

"Why don't you just worry about Demi and leave me out of it, okay?" He glared at his brother. "This happened at the resort. That's a little too close to home."

"Yeah. I thought that too." His brother was most likely thinking about Aylin. The last thing any of them wanted was for her to go through any more violence, though it didn't seem to impede her at all. She was actually using what happened to her in her latest book.

"What's the damage? And was Demi hurt at all?"

"No, whoever did this was already gone when she got here. It looks like they broke a window to get into the car, went through the boxes she had stored inside, and slashed a couple of her tires."

He took a closer look at the Jeep. Damn...one of the tires they slashed was the new one he just changed. And with two slashed, the car was not drivable. Not that she would want to with a window smashed either.

Glass and items from the boxes littered the ground around the vehicle. Someone really wanted to make a point, but what was that point? If it was to scare her, then they seemed to have done a pretty good job of it. But take this incident with the tire he took in where they found the bullet—that was way more than a coincidence.

Oliver vowed to himself to take care of Demi and to make sure nothing happened to her. The others would as well. But he was the one who practically lived next door, so it would be up to him to make sure she was safe, he thought as Luke and Demi walked over to him and Simon when they finished their conversation.

"What are you doing here?" Demi asked when he walked up to her and Luke.

"It looks like you've got another tire problem. I'm here to bring you home," he answered.

"I do seem to be having an issue keeping tires in one piece lately. I appreciate the ride home, but if you need to work, I can find another way home."

"I can drop you off on my way back to the station," Luke piped in from behind her with a smirk in Oliver's direction.

No way was he about to let that happen. The jerk was trying to rile him up. Sometimes he really hated being part of such a close family. They were always into each other's business.

"That's all right. I was finished for the day and heading home anyway. It's no trouble getting you home since we're going the same way."

Demi stood in front of him, her posture unsure with her arms wrapped around herself, and looked back and forth between him and Luke. "Since Oliver's going my way, I'll catch a ride back with him. No need for you to go out of your way for me, Luke."

"It's never out of the way for me, Demi-Lyn. Remember what I said," Luke reminded her. Oliver wished he knew what it was he had said to her that put such a serious look on both of their faces. Luke's was downright fierce, but Demi didn't look scared by it, more relieved than anything.

Oliver shared a look with Luke and Simon while directing Demi to his car. They had his and Demi's backs. But it would be up to him to make sure she stayed safe when she was at home. He only hoped whoever was after her got the hint that she was protected and left her alone.

9

Oliver steered Demi over to his car, making sure she was settled inside with her seatbelt on. She still looked to be in shock, but she also had a spine of steel. He was worried about her. She was trying to be so strong, but these last months—with the death of her parents, taking care of their house and business, quitting her job, moving to another state, and now having someone after her—it had to be putting some strain on her.

He realized he wanted to take care of her and always had. When did she become so important to him? He couldn't really pinpoint a specific time. Was it when she kissed him? Did she work her way into him over the years they were apart? Or was it because she was suddenly thrust in front of him for the first time in twelve years when she was stuck in the ditch?

Regardless of the reason, he didn't want anything to happen to her. He would do anything and everything to make sure she was safe. It was his duty as a friend and neighbor. Add in how he was starting to feel about her, and he had to protect her from whoever was doing this to her.

Oliver's gaze shifted to Demi moving something around in

her hands. Taking a quick glance, he realized they were rosary beads.

"Are those your mother's rosary beads?" he asked.

Oliver remembered seeing Malaya Shaw over the years pull them out of her pocket frequently. He had a brief memory of being at the resort beach, hanging out with his family and friends, and seeing her mother pull them out of her pocket as she sat talking to his mother. She carried them around with her everywhere. Unlike those that looked like a necklace or bracelet, these were more like a chain of five black beads—symbolizing grounding and protection he once heard her mother say—connected with short silver linked chains. One end had a silver cross, while the other held a centerpiece also made of silver. Demi's mother never went anywhere without them.

"Yeah. For some reason, I can't seem to let them go. They were with her all the time, so even though I took after my father and rarely go to church, I just couldn't part with her rosary beads. They were the last thing I have of her that was with her when she died." Demi said, her voice catching as she continued to fiddle with the rosary beads in her hands.

Something niggled at the back of his mind. Oliver was surprised to find Demi had the rosary beads. He imagined they wouldn't have survived after the way her parents died. From what he had heard from Katia, the car had been fully engulfed in flames when the police and fire department had arrived.

Since Demi's mother always kept the rosary beads in her pocket, he thought they wouldn't have survived the fire either. What did that mean? Were the rosary beads thrown out of the car in the crash before the car caught fire? He supposed they might have been, if Mrs. Shaw was holding them at the time of the crash. The impact that rendered them incapacitated may have also ripped them out of her hand and out of the car.

Oliver was satisfied with that theory. It made perfect sense to him and put his mind at ease.

"So now you hold them for her," he told her. It was hard to lose someone. Oliver lost his mother suddenly a year ago, and he was still working through the grief, yet she lost both her parents, and that was something he couldn't even imagine. He sometimes wished he had something that belonged to his mother, like Demi had from her mother, and he was sure she had from her father. Unfortunately, he wasn't ready to ask his father for something to remember her by. But he was getting closer.

"I guess I do," she said with a sad smile.

As they drove, Oliver tried to talk to her some more, but she was giving one-word answers, and he didn't really know what to say to her to make things better. So they continued to drive in silence until they got to her home.

Noticing their neighbor was outside, Oliver cursed. It would be difficult to avoid Mrs. Tepen as they tried to move inside from the car. The last thing he wanted to put her through was a talk with their nosy neighbor.

"Looks like we might need to appease Mrs. Tepen before we can go inside. You all right with that?" He asked.

"Yes, that's fine," she replied, nodding her head. Staring at her, Oliver realized it was not fine, yet he couldn't think of another way to avoid having to talk to the older woman.

"We'll make it as brief and quick as we can, okay?" he promised. "Stay here, and I'll come around." She nodded at him again, and he got out of the car, going around to the passenger side to open the door for Demi.

"Oliver, driving our Demi-Lyn home? Is something wrong?" Mrs. Tepen asked, stepping up to the fence line. She was the ultimate busybody, but the older woman was like a grandmother to him. Other than when he really didn't feel like talking. Like when Demi really wasn't up to it and he needed to make her comfortable inside. Or when he was running late for work. Or when he finally got home from a tiring day.

All right...so maybe she was the grandmother he only visited once a year. She would ply him with sweets the entire time, his parents trying to prevent him from going into a sugar coma by telling her he'd had enough, but being unable to stop her from slipping him a treat every time their backs were turned. Only to come home and puke his guts up later that night.

"Nothing to worry about, Mrs. Tepen. Demi's car just broke down, and I offered to give her a ride home. We need to call the auto shop, so we can't really talk right now. I'll come by this weekend, and maybe you'll have some of those wonderful cookies?" he asked, redirecting her thoughts away from Demi as he walked with her toward the front door.

"Oh yes! I'll make my special cookies just for you, Oliver. And maybe Demi-Lyn would like some, too? Just to make you feel better, you know."

"Of course, I would love some, Mrs. Tepen," Demi replied with a smile that didn't quite reach her eyes.

"Hand me your keys," he whispered to Demi. Taking them from her hand, he unlocked her door and ushered her in, waving to their neighbor before closing and locking the door.

He placed the key on the table beside the door and walked further inside. Turning his head, Oliver noted that Demi still hadn't moved from her spot at the front door. He went back and gently took her arm, walking her to the couch and gently getting her settled.

"Would you like a cup of tea or something?"

She rested her head on the back of the couch and closed her eyes. "No," she replied. He guessed she was in the mood just to sit without talking. He could do that.

Taking a seat in the chair next to the couch, Oliver kept his gaze on her as she rested. He didn't like the way she was just going along with little emotion. Like she was trying to close it all out.

He should know...he was a pro at holding his emotions in all the time. Of course, over time they still found a way out. Usually in the worst possible way. He had been working on that. He finally went to a therapist a few months ago to work through his grief. Again, he wasn't there yet, but he felt better than he had before he went.

He took Demi in some more. She looked pale too. And obviously tired. He wondered how much sleep she had gotten in the last seven months. Not much, by the looks of it. She was too thin, though it was possible that was how she normally looked, or maybe she had recently lost weight with all the stress and grief. He would need to ask Katia to be sure. She spoke to her all the time, including talking to her over video.

No matter what, Oliver planned to do something about it. He would definitely feed her. In the meantime, he would wait for as long as she needed him to until she was ready to talk about it.

But first he had to move his car before Mrs. Tepen started spreading rumors about them.

"Boss, what you wanted wasn't in the car."

"I don't care where it wasn't. Call me when you have it. Wrap it up, or you'll both be wishing for death if I need to step in to take care of it myself."

"Yes, sir. We're following her now. We'll get what is yours."

"Make sure you do."

The man hung up and looked at the man driving. "We need to find what the boss wants, or it's going to be our heads. No more playing around."

"Who's playing? We need to make sure the bitch gets it for all the trouble she's put us through."

The men followed Demi-Lyn Shaw and the man who drove her home. Parking down the street next to a park, they observed them interacting with the old lady next door. They would scrutinize her every move and those around her before making a plan.

The older woman would be a problem when they came back to the house. They needed to go through it to find what the bitch stole from their boss. The old lady seemed the type to pay attention to everything going on in the neighborhood. If needed, they would get rid of her, too. He wasn't one to care who he hurt as long as it wasn't him. He'd even throw his own mother out of a moving car if it meant saving himself.

No one would stand in their way of getting what Mr. Heaton wanted. And now, their own heads were on the line. They would enjoy taking care of anyone who got in their way if it meant living another day.

"We'll keep an eye out. We can sit here without raising too much suspicion, but we'll need to leave and move to another place later to avoid the woman from wondering why we're parked here for too long."

"As soon as we have the opportunity, we'll go in and find it in the house. I'd rather do it when the guy isn't around."

"Agreed."

The men continued to watch and plan their next move, noticing everything the woman next door to Demi-Lyn did and watching for the guy she came home with. They needed to have every little detail and routine memorized. The men would not fail in their mission to find what belonged to their boss.

10

Demi was feeling numb. Everything that happened today was culminating all at once inside of her. She couldn't erase it all from her mind, and it was starting to sink in that she wasn't safe. She rested her head against the back of the couch with her eyes closed.

Tired, Demi wished she'd just go to sleep and wake up with everything back to normal. What were they looking for in her Jeep? Or did someone hate her so much that they wanted to just destroy everything so completely? She wasn't sure she really wanted to have the answer to any of those questions.

The thought that someone local was targeting her left her with a nasty taste in her mouth. But why would it really be someone local? As far as she understood, the Kerrigans were the only people who were aware she was coming back. They wouldn't do anything like this to her. Ever.

So who else could it be? She thought back to when she was still in Maryland taking care of her parents' home, trying to think if anything odd had taken place then. She remembered nothing, but she was so distraught over losing her parents that she probably wouldn't have noticed.

But there was that one time she thought someone had been in the house.

It was after she had boxed everything up already and temporarily moved the trailer to a storage facility to keep it all safe until she was ready to leave. She had walked into the house to do a final walk-through and to meet the realtor to have pictures taken for the listing, give her a key, and sign the paperwork. The realtor had not arrived yet, but the hair on the back of her neck was standing on end, as if someone was in the house with her. Being in the house by herself made her uneasy and nervous. It was already eerie being in the house without her parents and half empty, with excess furniture covered up. She thought it was her imagination, but then she heard a creak coming from the back of the house. As she was about to investigate, the realtor arrived, and she no longer felt uncomfortable.

They never found anyone in the house as they went through it.

And now here she was in Cypress Bay, and it was happening all over again. It must be because Oliver was still sitting with her and not talking. She sensed him sitting nearby, staring at her. He'd left for a moment, a slice of disappointment hitting her square in the chest. But then he came back, closing and locking the door behind him before sitting in the chair to resume his study of her.

Occasionally he'd take a deep breath before letting it out, as though he was trying to calm himself down. She remembered he had a hard time when they were younger keeping himself calm. He must have learned some breathing techniques to help him relax. They sounded like the ones she learned when she went to the therapist in Maryland after her parents died.

She was having a hard time and really needed to talk to someone who wasn't a friend of hers or her parents, a co-worker, the priest from her mother's church, or anyone else who heard what happened. The therapist gave her a safe place to talk it all out. She was still grieving, but she made it through each day better than the last.

Everyone else in her life treated her with kid gloves. Oh, her friends and her parents' friends meant well. They just didn't understand how to handle someone who was grieving over a sudden loss. Only instead of taking the time to sit with her and letting her work through that loss, they treated her as though she was made of glass and was going to break.

She hated that.

But she proved she was strong enough to make it. Even if they thought she was making a drastic change to her life without taking the time to process everything. Yet it wasn't about them. She had to leave Maryland. Her friends were not really friends. They were more like acquaintances. She hung out with them, but they really didn't know her. She hated her job. Her apartment was a white box, a place for her to sleep and live, but it wasn't her. It wasn't really that hard to leave. Without her parents, there was nothing left for her.

Demi noticed Oliver doing the same thing—treating her like she was made of glass—and yet he was also here, not saying anything, letting her work through what happened earlier. That he was doing the one thing others would not—quietly supporting her—was another reason she felt close to him.

Katia thought her crush on him was gone, but what she didn't realize was that Demi never had a crush on Oliver. She loved him. Sure, she had no idea what that meant when she was fourteen years old. Maybe back then it was merely a crush.

But over the years, even though she hadn't seen him in the last twelve years, Demi had heard about what he was doing. How he went to culinary school and was at the top of his class. How he went to Europe during the summers to study different cooking techniques. And then how he came back to Cypress

Bay to work at the resort, taking over the kitchen as the head chef and manager, eschewing the many offers that came from some of the top restaurants in the world. He had opportunities to work in Paris, London, or New York City. Instead, he came home.

And that was yet another reason she loved him. Not that she'd ever tell him. He did no more than tolerate her as a kid. Another girl hanging around his cousins to watch over and protect. He and the other boys made it their business to include her in their protection of Katia, Marinda, Ryleigh, and Hailee. Now that she thought about it, they also included Emma Cooper, who was local and good friends with Ryleigh. Her brother, Sean, hung out with Noah and Luke, while Joel Madris hung out with Simon.

Growing up, she wished her parents had moved down to Cypress Bay permanently, so she'd be there year round. The only consolation was that she was there now. Even if it took her parents dying for it to happen.

Demi silently sighed. What was she doing simply sitting on the couch? She was wallowing in past grief and what could have been instead of living. The recent incidents should have moved her to live.

No one ever knew how much time they had.

That much she had learned in the months since her parents' deaths. She needed to feel something. She needed Oliver. Demi may have always wanted him—loved him—but now she needed him to feel alive after what had happened since arriving in Cypress Bay. If she asked him to spend the night, would he resist her? After everything going on, Demi didn't want to experience pity or any type of rejection from him.

Without opening her eyes, she said, "Oliver, I need you."

"I'm right here, Demi, what do you need?" he whispered from the chair to her right.

Demi didn't want to open her eyes or look at him yet. She couldn't survive it if he didn't understand. "You."

"Do you need a drink? I can make you something to eat," he asked in concern.

Why couldn't Oliver understand what she was trying to say without her needing to spell it out for him? She just needed to feel something. And she wanted to feel it with him.

It had been so long since Demi had slept with a man. She had always hoped that Oliver would have been her first, but that wasn't meant to be. That didn't mean she couldn't have him now. Right? Was it too outrageous to think he might want her as much as she wanted him? Demi didn't think so.

Opening her eyes to stare at him, Demi showed him everything she was feeling—all the pain, all the desire, all the love. "Stop trying to feed me. I need you!"

11

"What do you want me to do, Demi?" he asked, curious about what she was looking for from him.

Oliver didn't understand what Demi meant by needing him at first. What did she want from him? She seemed so fragile when he first spotted her in the resort parking lot and then when they got to her home, where she all but collapsed onto the couch. Did she need him to talk to her, comfort her, be a sounding board for her to let it all out? He would do whatever it took to make her seem more like herself.

The confident young woman was a little lost, yet strong as hell. She was always like that, even as a kid. "Headstrong," her father would always say in the most loving way possible. She was definitely her father's daughter. She may have the look of her mother, but her personality was the spitting image of her father.

He didn't think she was going to answer his question until she opened those beautiful brown eyes, exposing all that emotion, all that need, all that want. And that those emotions, needs, and wants were directed at him, it blew him away. Jump-started his heart to beat in double time. And Oliver knew...he would not come out of this unscathed, and even knowing that, he would do anything for Demi. He would do anything for her, even if it meant destroying himself in the process.

"I want you," she said again, "I need to feel."

So much emotion rolled off her that Oliver wasn't sure he'd be able to do anything but comfort her in any way that she needed. Despite the hit he was going to take to his head and heart once this was all over, he couldn't help the thrill of having every part of her.

Still, he needed to make sure she spelled it out for him. Oliver didn't want any miscommunication between them. His mind had been going to every dirty thing he wanted to do to her ever since he came across her again. For all he knew, Demi meant she wanted him to hold her or stay on the couch to protect her through the night. No, he definitely needed some clarification on what Demi meant when she said she needed him.

"And I need to understand exactly what you mean, Demi. Spell it out for me," he demanded. If she wanted all the things he was thinking about doing to her, then she'd need to tell him that was the direction she wanted to go with him.

Demi slowly got up from the couch, walked over to him, climbed into his lap and straddled him. Well, that certainly cleared things up. Oliver thought it was a marvelous idea, but thought the timing was off for Demi. Was she doing this for the right reasons?

Would she regret it later? Should he say the hell with it and go for it? Deal with the fallout later? Or would he also regret it in the morning? "Are you sure? You won't regret this in the morning?" he asked carefully.

He just realized that he wanted her...was it too soon for sex? But he also experienced what it was like losing someone close to him and the numbness running through his body. Demi was still dealing with the death of her parents and then the vandalism to her vehicle on top of it. She uprooted her whole life, and nothing seemed to go back together again. Was this right for them?

"I'm sure. I've been thinking about this ever since I saw you again on the side of the road," she replied.

He didn't think she realized she was grinding herself against him. Her core kept moving over his cock, making him lose his mind. He needed her to hurry and tell him exactly what she wanted. "This?"

"Sex, Oliver," she whispered into his ear, making him want to shiver all over. "Right now, all night. Fuck me, Oli."

Damn. How did he get so lucky? A twinge of guilt, like he was taking advantage of her, was still pinging in his head, but he quickly squashed it. She was persistent about wanting to have sex with him, grinding on him more and more. His control was quickly waning with every movement she made on his lap. The last straw was when she swirled her tongue around his ear before sucking his earlobe into her mouth, letting it out with a soft pop.

He stood abruptly, holding Demi in his arms. Her legs wrapped around his waist, her arms around his neck...the same neck she was currently moving her tongue over in small little licks. Damn it! She was driving him fucking crazy! Oliver briskly walked out of the living room and down the hallway.

"Which room?" he asked, desperate to find a bed. He would not last otherwise, and he didn't want to take her against the wall. At least not yet.

"The last door at the end."

Opening the door, he registered that it was the master bedroom. For some reason, he thought she would still be in her old room, not ready to move into her parents' room yet. That just showed him again how strong she really was. She may struggle with their deaths, but she didn't let that stop her from making their house hers, to start moving on to create a life for herself.

He took in the changes to the room. The last time he was in the house was about five months ago, a couple of months after the Shaws died. His aunt and uncle were probably aware Demi would eventually be down and wanted him to give everything a quick look for them. Back then, the bed was made up with her mother's flower-print comforter and a ton of pillows. He never understood how Mr. Shaw put up with it all.

He had asked him once and was told that when a man loved a woman as much as he loved his wife, you'd do anything to make her happy. He said that, marrying him took her away from her home to a new country, the least he could do was let her decorate the house any way she wanted.

Now the room had a more laid-back look to it. Something he suspected even her father would have preferred over the flowery decor and mountain of pillows. The bed had two pillows, one on either side of the bed, and the comforter was a plain checkered pattern in blues, greens, and reds. He wasn't surprised that Demi liked a more masculine look to her bedroom. She had always been more tomboy than girly.

Laying her out over the bed, Oliver couldn't wait to unwrap her. He had equal parts of excitement and dread at the prospect of running through his body. Once they did this, could they even go back to how things were before? Would he even want them to? He quickly shut those thoughts down. He would not let the thoughts inside his own head rule this moment. He had a beautiful woman, all lean and willowy, in a bed, waiting for him to devour her.

12

"The things I've thought about doing to you. Are you sure this is what you want, Demi?"

Demi couldn't believe she was about to have sex with Oliver. Finally! And then he had to be all dirty and concerned at the same time. What the hell? She just wanted him to ravish her, make her forget all of her problems for one night. Was that too much to ask? She didn't want him to worry about what she thought. She just wanted him to fuck her.

Weren't guys supposed to be thinking about sex all the time...trying to get inside a woman's pants any way possible? Of course she would want the one guy who was responsible and wanted to make sure she was all right with it. She had been waiting for him, it seemed, for her entire life. Now that the waiting was finally over...he wanted to take his time with reassurance? No, that would not work for her. She wanted more action, less talking, unless it was the dirty kind.

She looked up at him hovering over her. "I want you to do all the things you've thought about. No holding back, Oliver."

"Oh, sweetheart, I'm not sure you realize what you're getting yourself into."

"I think I do. Less talking, more fucking." Demi's mother would have lectured her for hours with all of her swearing. Her father would have just given her a look. Not because he thought it was rude to swear—he swore more than she did—but because her mother didn't like it. Oliver apparently didn't feel the same if the hungry look on his face was to be believed. He looked as though he were a tiger ready to pounce on his prey.

She couldn't wait.

His hands moved to cup her face, his fingers digging into her hair. Oliver leaned down and devoured her. There was no other word for the kiss he gave her...no took from her. Their first kiss was as innocent as she was at fourteen, a hard peck on the lips, no open mouths, no tongues, just a quick meeting of lips. Compared to that, this was a claiming. He owned every part of her mouth, nipping at her lips, running his tongue over hers and around her mouth. The kiss was passionate and brought her back to life.

Their first adult kiss.

She gripped his forearms as he held onto her. Demi needed to ground herself or she was going to fly away with the pleasure he was giving her with just this kiss.

As quickly as he had started the kiss, Oliver pulled his mouth away without letting her go. They were both breathing heavily—as though at the end of a marathon—their breaths mingling. Their chests were rising and falling in rapid unison. Shallow breaths didn't give Demi enough air to flow into her lungs, but she didn't care. She'd do it all again for another kiss like that.

"Demi, be sure," he implored her.

She searched his gaze. The lust and desire were swirling deep in his eyes, but he also had a hint of vulnerability. He wasn't sure about this any more than she was, yet she needed him desperately. There was no other man for her. He was it, even if it never lasted past tonight.

"I'm sure, Oliver," she told him. His look changed from vulnerable and unsure to predatory in a blink, the lust and desire taking over completely.

He released his hands from her face and hair, sliding them down around her jaw, her neck, to the collar of her shirt. He lightly moved his fingers down the center, tracing on either side of the buttons. Grabbing the fabric just below her breasts, Demi gasped as Oliver gave a tug, ripping the shirt apart, buttons flying in all directions. Before making sense of it, he released the center clasp of her bra and had his mouth on her nipple, sucking it in deep and hard. She cried out at the small amount of discomfort and the immense pleasure that reached all the way to her clit. It was intoxicating and something she'd never experienced before.

"More. I need more," she cried out, her hands clenching in his hair.

Oliver moved to her other nipple, treating it in the same way. She couldn't take anymore, and yet she didn't want him to stop. Demi was going to explode just from what he was doing to her breasts. Before she climaxed, he released her nipple.

"No!" Now she'd never have an orgasm. Once she started, it had to continue, or she was done. It had always been that way in the past.

Disappointment built as he began kissing down her torso while releasing the button on her pants.

She had dressed up in a nice button-down shirt and dress slacks for her meeting with Simon. A pair of jeans and a t-shirt would have been fine—it was Simon after all—but she wanted to treat it as a job interview and do it right.

Now she wanted them off. She wondered what else Oliver had in store for her. Helping him remove her pants and panties, she kicked them off when they got to her ankles. Demi had no idea where her shoes had gone. Did she take them off at the door? Or did Oliver take them off with her pants?

"I can tell I need to step things up. You're thinking and we can't have that," he muttered right before he put the tip of his tongue on her clit, licking it in tiny circles.

Her mind immediately went blank with the sensations bombarding her as he licked, sucked, and nipped at her clit. Shoes? Who cared about her shoes? Demi screamed as the climax she thought long gone suddenly hit her, immediately going boneless with exhaustion.

Her whole body was more relaxed than it had ever been before. It was like she was a pile of mush, puddled in the middle of the bed.

"Don't fall asleep on me now, Demi. The best is yet to come," Oliver teased. She couldn't remember the last time she had heard him teasing anyone. He was always so serious...or angry.

She glimpsed him through slitted eyes. He swiftly removed his clothes, took a condom out of his wallet, and then just as quickly put it on. She lifted her arms to him as he came down over her, wrapping them around him to grip the back of his shoulders.

Oliver rested on his elbows at her head, giving her a deep kiss as he slowly inched his cock inside of her. He was going too slow for her. Where did the fast-paced Oliver go?

With a burst of renewed energy, Demi took matters into her own hands. She wrapped her legs around his waist, crossing her ankles below his butt, and pulled herself up and him down, forcing him completely inside her.

"Demi," he growled in warning, as he remained still inside her no matter how much she tried to make him move.

"Oliver, please," she begged him with words, imploring him with her eyes to move. After a tense stare-down, Oliver relented and rocked into her. "Harder. Faster. Oh!"

Oliver increased his speed, shuttling in and out of her faster, harder, and deeper. Hanging on was the only thing she was able to do as he finally lost the control he tried to hold on to tightly. Her hands grasped for purchase on his back. His mouth came down, sucking on her neck, licking up to the spot behind her ear that was more sensitive than she realized.

Demi heard him breathing heavily in her ear, his mouth resting against the edge of her cheek. "You're wrapped around my cock so tight. I can't hold on much longer. Make yourself come, Demi."

She removed one arm from around him, moving her hand between them to flick her fingers over her clit. Her orgasm was building, tighter and tighter; she was almost afraid to keep going. She'd never had two in one night before.

"No, don't stop. Do not stop unless I tell you to." His demand made her hotter than she had ever been before. It was impossible for her to stop now. She was compelled to continue.

Faster and faster he moved in her until she couldn't take it anymore, breaking with an orgasm that seemed to go on forever as she screamed out in ecstasy.

"Demi. Oh. That's it, sweetheart, keep your orgasm going, don't stop. You're squeezing me so hard." Oliver stroked in her one, two, three more times before he was calling out her name again.

Oliver trapped her hand under him as he collapsed on top of her. She shivered at his weight on her. It was so good. Comfortable.

Demi could get used to having Oliver in her bed, making him lose control with her, even when he didn't want to. The orgasms didn't hurt, either. She'd never been so relaxed in her life. Now she understood why guys passed out after sex. She was so satiated.

She groaned as he shifted off her, pulling out of her body. "Be right back," he said.

He walked naked into her bathroom without turning on the lights. After hearing the toilet flush and the water in the sink run, then turn off, he walked back to the bed, climbing in beside her.

Pulling her into his embrace, he pulled the blanket up over them. "Sleep," he demanded.

When did he become so bossy? And why did she like it so much? Too tired to respond to him or herself, her last thought before falling asleep was that Oliver was supposed to be with her...forever.

13

Early the next morning, Oliver slowly woke. What was the weight resting on his left arm and shoulder? As he became more aware of his surroundings, he remembered he had stayed the night with Demi.

Everything they did together came crashing into him; a blush crept up over his chest and face at how forceful he was with her. Of course, she didn't seem to mind, and that had the blush receding.

Oliver enjoyed being in control. It wasn't something he had done in past relationships. Though looking back, many of them weren't exactly healthy or with someone he cared about. Many of the women were too busy building their own careers or used him to get ahead, thinking he somehow had sway with the owners of the restaurants or something. He didn't. And when they realized that for themselves, many left to find their next conquest. It was a chaotic time in his life, and Oliver admitted he wasn't really looking for a permanent relationship back then either.

Looking down, Demi was curled up next to him, her hands pressed to his side, her left leg thrown over his. She looked so peaceful. He was happy she was, since he imagined she wasn't getting much sleep lately. Not with the loss of her parents still so new along with what had been happening to her since coming back to Cypress Bay.

His own reactions were a surprise, though. He wasn't panicking at still being in her bed. And he didn't feel any regret about sleeping with her...or having sex with her for that matter.

They'd turned to each other a couple more times in the night. Each time better than the first. The first time, he woke her up with his mouth on her pussy. He devoured her with his tongue and lips, concluding that she was the best-tasting dessert he'd ever had.

The second time, she surprised him with her mouth wrapped around his cock. Before he got the upper hand, Demi did some sort of twisting thing with her hand right below her mouth, and he shot off like a teenager having his first sexual experience. It was both disconcerting and amazing at the same time.

Being with her was fun, exciting, and easy. Oliver loved every moment of the night with her. He'd need to think about what that meant for him. He wasn't sure he was ready for a permanent relationship with her. Or anyone, for that matter. His life was chaotic running the kitchen and restaurants at Cypress Manor. He'd be a terrible boyfriend since he was always working. And when he wasn't at the resort, he was working on new recipes at home.

Emotionally, he sure as hell wasn't good enough for Demi. She needed someone who didn't let his emotions build until his temper blew everything up. It had always been his problem, which only became worse once his paternal grandparents passed away when the pandemic hit, and then his mother was killed a few years later by a drunk driver.

Oliver had a tendency to hold in all of his emotions until they couldn't be contained any longer and blew out of him faster than a speeding train. It was something he'd been working on recently. He didn't want to be 'stone cold' as his brother and cousins frequently thought of him.

He was furious when he spotted Demi's car in the resort parking lot yesterday. So much so that he was ready to haul off and kill the men who had the nerve to destroy her Jeep and everything in it. But being around her calmed him down considerably. It was like she completed him in some way...and wasn't that something else to think about.

Seeing her try to keep in all the fear she was experiencing at yet another attack on her while at the resort, and then how she succumbed to the shock, only to rally back and ask him to sleep with her—if given the chance to be with her again, he'd take it. Not that he wanted only sex. No, he'd be with her anyway she'd let him. And that was another thing he needed to think about, he thought with a sigh.

Now though he had to figure out a way to untangle himself from Demi without waking her up. He needed to make a quick trip to the bathroom, then grab another condom because he knew exactly how he wanted to wake Demi up this morning. Oliver slowly extricated himself from her. She didn't move at all. If he didn't view her chest moving in and out every time she took a breath, he would think she had died in her sleep...she was that still.

Just as Oliver finished up in the bathroom and grabbed a condom from his pants lying on the floor, the doorbell rang, followed by a banging on the door. Who the hell was ringing and banging on the front door so early? He looked over at Demi. Surely all that noise would wake her up, but she was still sleeping soundly.

Shaking his head at that, he was slightly miffed that the person on the other side of the door was ruining his chance at a morning tryst. Oliver shook Demi to wake her up.

"Go away," she mumbled.

"Demi, there's someone at the door," he said softly.

"I'll get up in a minute," she said as she fell back asleep.

He shrugged before putting on his pants and went to answer the door sans shirt. Upon opening the door, he was surprised to see Katia, though he shouldn't have been. Demi and Katia had always been good friends, so it stood to reason that they would pick up right where they left off.

Katia's mouth hung open, her eyes practically bugging out of her head at him standing in front of her answering the door. He shouldn't enjoy that so much, but considering she disturbed his morning plans with Demi, he figured the more shocked the better.

"Good morning, Katia. What brings you by so early?" he asked, amused as she opened and closed her mouth several times. "Demi's still sleeping, so why don't you come in and I'll try to wake her up."

When Katia didn't move from the door, Oliver gently took her hand and pulled her inside, closing the door behind her. No need to ignite Mrs. Tepen's curiosity with him standing in the doorway half dressed. She often spent much of the morning staring out her windows, while having her morning coffee, getting an early start on the comings and goings of the neighborhood.

Katia's mouth was finally closed, but she still hadn't made a sound at finding him in Demi's house. He figured she'd make sense of what he was doing in only a pair of pants soon enough. Before that happened though, Demi walked out of the bedroom, coming to a halt when she noticed Katia.

Oliver was thankful she had decided to put some clothes on. They went to bed naked, which came in handy when they turned to each other throughout the night. She now had on a pair of sleep shorts and a tank top. Looking at her in them made him hard instantly. Now if Katia would just leave, he'd take Demi back to bed and show her how hard she made him.

With the two of them standing still, staring at each other, Oliver suspected it would not happen.

He needed to give them time to talk, and he needed to go into work.

"I'm going to grab my shirt and head home. I need to get ready for work," he told them, walking past a still frozen-in-place Demi to the bedroom.

Once in the bedroom, he picked up his shirt, throwing it on as he walked back down the hallway. He was amused that they hadn't moved an inch while he was away.

He kissed Demi hard and deep. "I'll see you later," Oliver said as he walked out the door, closing it behind him.

14

"What was that?"

Demi shook herself out of her early morning stupor. It was too early for whatever had just happened. She looked over at Katia, the front door, then back at Katia.

How did she explain Oliver being in her house so early to her best friend? They talked about everything. Katia was the one person Demi went to whenever she needed to talk things out. So why was she having such a hard time trying to explain Oliver being half-dressed this morning and the kiss he gave her on his way out?

"What was Oliver doing here half-dressed this morning? No, wait! I need coffee first," Katia said as she started walking to Demi's kitchen. "If this is going where I think it's going, then I need a healthy dose of caffeine, and I know you aren't even awake yet. That's my cousin we're about to talk about coming out of your room and answering the door with no shirt on and his pants unbuttoned. Ewww...okay, I don't want what I expect are sex details...because again...ewww. He is my cousin. He's like a big brother, really. So the last thing I need are those types of details, but what the hell, Demi?"

Demi followed her into the kitchen as she continued rambling. Katia measured out the coffee into the pot before pouring water in. She got everything else out that was needed for their coffee. Cups, spoons, sugar, cream...even a couple of plates with some cookies. Where did she get the cookies?

Demi had a hard time keeping up with her. She was talking more like her sister, Ryleigh, who talked a mile a minute—anything and everything coming out of her mouth without much of a filter. Obviously, being a triplet had some characteristics rub off on each of them occasionally.

"His car wasn't in your driveway when Mrs. Tepen stopped me to give me the cookies. But then Oliver was standing in front of me when the door opened and..." Katia rambled on as Demi stopped listening.

She was too tired to really catch half of what she said, but Demi did her best as she sat down. "Hey, Katia. What brings you by?"

"That's where you want to start, huh?"

Demi stared at Katia until the other woman sighed. She turned to pour their coffee from the half-filled carafe, the coffee still brewing and spitting drops on the hot plate before she replaced it back to collect the remaining brew. Placing the cups down in front of them, Katia took a seat across from her, doctored up her coffee and took a sip before resuming the conversation.

"Marinda called last night and told me about your Jeep. I wanted to come by then, but I had to close up the shop, and it was late by the time I got home. Are you okay?"

"I'm not sure what to think about everything that's going on, Katia."

"Are you talking about the vandalism or Oliver?"

"Both?" Demi looked down and realized her coffee was still sitting in front of her on the table. Fixing it up, she took a sip before continuing. "The vandalism wasn't the first thing that happened. On the first day I got here, my tire blew out. Oliver was driving by and stopped to help. He offered to take the tire to have it repaired, but they found a bullet in the tire."

"What! You were shot at? Why am I just now hearing about this?" Katia asked sadly.

"I thought it wasn't that big of a deal. I mean, obviously being shot at is not good, but Luke thought it may have been a stray bullet from a hunter or something...maybe. He wasn't sure. But then with what happened at the resort..."

"It now seems to be a pattern, like something else is going on," Katia continued for her.

Nodding her head, Demi took another small sip of her coffee. "I'm sorry, Katia, for not calling you. Last night was a bit of a shock, you know? What they did to the Jeep and the stuff I had in it took some genuine anger. Why would they be angry with me?"

"I don't know, but if Luke is taking care of it, then he'll figure it out," she said confidently. "What I really want to find out is what's up with you and Oliver. You've had a crush on him forever."

"A crush...come on, that may have been true when we were kids, but not anymore," she protested. "I just needed to feel alive and whole after everything that happened. I'm not in a place where I can have a relationship, and definitely not with Oliver."

"What's wrong with Oliver?"

"Nothing. Really. I just don't think it's wise to start a relationship so soon after I lost my parents and all these other things are happening to me, too. Besides, you told me before that he was still having problems dealing with his mother's death. It wouldn't be something he would want either."

"Okay. I'll curb my impulses to keep on asking about the two of you...for now."

"Thank you." Demi wouldn't be able to hold Katia off forever, but she was still confused about what she felt about

Oliver. Sex with him was spectacular. Who knew Oliver was a dirty talker during sex? Or that he took charge like her favorite book boyfriend. She liked it. Too much. It would be nice to talk about it with someone...just not yet.

"What are you going to do with all the stuff you have piled up from your parents?"

"I've been putting a lot up in the attic. I need to move some more of it. The attic is getting kind of full, though. I didn't realize how much stuff I really had, plus whatever was already in this house. I'll need to go through it all and decide what to keep and what to donate or throw away."

The women continued to talk about more lighthearted topics until Katia needed to go back to her shop.

"Come into town and The Lunch Counter sometime soon," Katia said. "I may not have a lot of time, but I can spare some to eat lunch with you in my office."

"I will. As soon as I have my Jeep back." She hoped that would be soon. It wasn't just the shock of her things lying scattered around the ground that upset her about the incident. It was that her father's Jeep was damaged. The SUV was a link to her father, and not having it around reminded her he wasn't with her anymore.

With Katia gone, she closed the door and flicked her mother's rosary beads through her fingers. They were her link to her mother. The one thing that was with her at all times and gave her the memories she needed to go on without her. That they were found at the crash scene and survived—despite the fire that killed her parents—was just the kind of miracle her mother always told her about growing up.

Demi looked around the vacation home they'd left her again. She really did need to go through all the boxes. But she was still in the clothes she had thrown on when she realized Oliver was no longer in bed and she heard talking from the other room. Demi wouldn't be able to start on the boxes until she showered and dressed.

Walking down the hall and into the bedroom, she got a little jolt from the unmade bed. She'd had sex with Oliver last night!

It was both surreal and exhilarating to think about. Demi was unsure what the future held when it came to Oliver, but she liked that he didn't pull away when Katia showed up. He walked right up to her when she came out of the bedroom and kissed her right in front of his cousin. She wondered if it meant anything or if he was just messing with Katia, but Demi'd take whatever he'd give her.

And wasn't that a sad thought? If only she were able to figure out what he was thinking. It was both a blessing and a curse that Katia showed up when she did. Demi didn't need to have an awkward morning—well, not more awkward than her friend catching her with Oliver. But she also could not wake up with him still in bed with her either.

With one wistful look back at the bed, Demi went into the bathroom and closed the door. It was time to prepare for the day. She had a mile-long list of things to do. Thinking about Oliver would need to wait.

15

As soon as he stepped out of Demi's house, he groaned. It was like Mrs. Tepen had a built-in radar or something. She was standing on her front porch waiting for him with a covered plate.

"Here are some cookies for you, dear. I sent another plate in with Katia for Demi-Lyn. I know you need to go to work, so I won't keep you. I trust our Demi-Lyn is all right?" she innocently asked.

Innocent? Mrs. Tepen was anything but innocent. He understood exactly what she was asking. She wanted him to confirm he had spent the night with Demi. Not bloody likely.

"Thank you for the cookies, Mrs. Tepen. Yes, Demi is all right. I'm running late, so I'll talk to you later."

"Yes, of course, dear. I'm sure you want to take a shower and change your clothes. Have a good day," she said with a twinkle of amusement.

She was cagey; he'd give her that.

Oliver made his getaway back to his home and got ready for the day after placing the cookies on the kitchen counter. Taking one for the road on his way out, he was glad he had the foresight to move his car back to his own driveway after getting Demi inside her house. When he got back, she was still sitting in the same place. He wasn't even sure she was aware he'd left for a moment.

Strolling into work, Oliver was determined to immediately seek out his brother. Demi needed a car, and since the vandalism occurred on their property, they should be the ones to order a car for her. If Simon wasn't willing to do it, then he'd take care of it. He didn't want her to be stuck at home ruminating over what was going on.

Knowing his brother would be in his office, he headed there first. It wasn't unusual for him to be in the office early in the morning and stay late into the night, especially since he lived on the property. But since meeting Aylin, Simon had tended to go home much earlier than usual. He still got to the office early, though. Mostly because Aylin said he was a pest while she tried to work on her latest book. It worked for them.

Giving a quick knock, he waited for Simon to tell him to come in. Once, when Simon and Aylin were still in the beginning stages of their relationship, Oliver had walked right into the office and caught them in a heavy make out session. The last thing he wanted to do was interrupt them again. Aylin sometimes visited during her breaks to catch up with Simon throughout the day.

At the command to come in, Oliver opened the door and looked around. "Is the coast clear?"

Simon smirked at him. "It is now."

He absolutely didn't want to know. "I need you to call a rental company to order Demi a car until hers is available again. Since her Jeep was damaged on our property, we should cover the cost of getting a rental car."

"I agree, and I was already going to ask you what she would prefer to drive when you got to work."

"How would I know what she would prefer to drive? Just

order her some wheels and maybe have Marinda bring it by or something."

Simon looked at him with amusement. "What? What's so bloody funny, Simon?" Damn, now he was sounding like his mother. The British colloquialisms he grew up with always popped out whenever he was getting pissed off or stressed. And Simon had the instruction manual on how to push all his buttons.

"Did you know Demi had a crush on you when she was a kid?" Simon asked.

Narrowing his eyes at him, Oliver told him, "I didn't at first, but she kissed me when I was seventeen."

Ha! That shocked him silent.

"She kissed you? She was only fourteen back then," Simon accused.

"Yeah, well...she surprised me, too. I was walking back to the resort parking lot to go home. She ran up and kissed me and then took off to go back to her parents. They left the next morning for Maryland, and I was about to go to culinary school. I took those summer cooking trips, and then she stopped coming with her parents for a while. So it was a true kiss and run. I haven't seen her in all those years. Once I moved into my house, I heard stories about her life from her parents. Her father would go on and on about what Demi was doing."

"I don't even know where to begin with all that. Where was I that summer?"

"You and Joel had gone on some trip. Backpacking or something before the next term started."

"That's right. What a summer that was," Simon said, reminiscing. "So what now?"

"What now?" Oliver pretended not to grasp what Simon was talking about. They may be a couple of years apart, but they had always been close growing up. They were each able to identify when the other was holding something back. And by the look Simon was giving him, Oliver wasn't fooling him at all. "I think I love her and always have. Now I just need to be sure and convince her once I am."

"Good luck with that. Speaking from experience, prepare to grovel when you stuff it up," Simon advised.

"I'm not you," he replied, knowing full well that Simon had the right of it. He wasn't even sure he loved Demi. He had just never felt this deep-seated need for another person before, and surely that must be love. Considering he was still trying to deal with his own shit—along with everything Demi was dealing with—told him it may not be the right time anyway. But he'd go with it and discover how it played out.

On Oliver's way out, Simon told him he would make sure Demi had a rental car that morning. Thanking him, he went to his kitchen to make sure everything was running smoothly, then into the office to work—with Demi and the night they spent together still on his mind.

What was it about her that drew him in? The last time he'd seen her, she was only a kid. If he were being honest, they were both kids back then. He may have been seventeen and thought he was so grown up—too grown up for Demi—but he comprehended nothing. The chaste kiss she gave him back then was the best he'd ever experienced.

Until last night.

Their kisses were explosive. And then they made love... Oliver now understood why some said sex was better with an emotional connection with the person they were with. He'd experienced nothing like what he had last night. He wasn't usually a take-charge kind of guy in bed, either. But something about Demi just brought it all out. It was exciting being with her, and he couldn't help himself. That she enjoyed herself and how he was with her made it all the better. He felt more like himself after last night than he ever had.

Until he started thinking too much about what it all meant.

Then, he was a ball of confusion because Demi was only fourteen years old the last time he'd seen her. All gangly legs and braces. Now she was a grown woman looking exactly like who he always imagined would be in his life. It was like his subconscious had told him all along she was it for him.

And that confused the bloody hell out of him. Maybe he was just like his brother. Heaving out a sigh, Oliver was going to stuff it up like Simon said.

Maybe he should prepare his groveling now, he thought with a chuckle. Look at him, preparing to mess up his relationship with Demi before it was even a relationship.

Shaking his head, he cleared his mind as much as possible and continued working on the paperwork. He wanted to get it done so he could get back on the kitchen floor, where he was the most comfortable. Maybe then he would stop thinking about Demi so much.

16

As the boxes started dwindling in the corner of the dining and living rooms, Demi glanced out the window when a couple of cars pulled up—one in her driveway and the other at the curb. She had never seen either of the cars before, though she hadn't been in town long enough to know what everyone was driving now.

The car in the driveway was what she would consider a luxury car...it was black and sleek and looked like it cost a lot more than she had ever made in her lifetime so far. The other car was also nice, but looked to be more worn and used.

Marinda got out of the luxury car, and another woman exited the car at the curb. They walked up the driveway to the front door together as Demi opened it for them.

"Hey Demi. Simon wanted you to have a rental car while you're waiting for yours to be fixed. I volunteered to bring it to you," Marinda told her before Demi even got a word out.

"And I needed to escape the apartment for a while, so I volunteered to bring Marinda back to the inn," the other woman said.

She didn't understand what was going on. The car Marinda was driving was hers? "He wanted me to have a rental car?"

"Yours was damaged on our property, so we all decided it was best to take care of the rental for you. Plus Oliver wanted to make sure you had a way to get around town," Marinda added.

Oliver was part of this, too? Wait, did Marinda say all of them decided it was best? "Who are all of you? And I'm sorry, but who are you?" she asked the woman with Marinda.

"Oh, that's right, you haven't met before. Demi, this is Aylin Miller. She's engaged to Simon and is a writer. Aylin, this is Demi-Lyn Shaw, but don't call her Demi-Lyn...only a few can get away with it. There was this time..."

"Okay...that's enough of that," she said, holding up her hand and cutting Marinda off. No one needed to hear how she went off on that poor guy who dared to call her Demi-Lyn.

And Marinda was right. She really only let a few people get away with calling her by her full name. Mrs. Tepen was one. Mostly because she had lived next door to the summer home forever, and she didn't have the heart to change it with her now. Not that she expected Mrs. Tepen would listen to her anyway, she thought wryly.

Luke Kerrigan also managed to say her full name without a penalty. She tried once to get him to stop, but he just steamrolled right over her...ignored her request and continued to call her Demi-Lyn instead of Demi with that damn smirk on his face. The jerk, she thought affectionately. Luke did it to rile her up, but she refused to let him. Over time, she got used to it.

"That's an interesting name." Aylin said.

"Yeah, well, my parents couldn't agree on a name when I was born. My father wanted to call me Demi, and my mother wanted to call me Lyn. Instead of fighting about it, they combined them."

All her life, her father insisted on calling her Demi. He was a big Demi Moore fan. She didn't understand why, but he watched every one of her movies.

Her mother insisted on calling her Lyn after her late grandmother, but they would both introduce her to others as Demi-Lyn. It was really confusing for a while growing up, especially at school or when her friends came over. After a while, everyone got used to it.

She didn't mind her full name, but it was a mouthful. Since middle school, she had decided she preferred to be called Demi, much to the chagrin of her mother.

They talked a little more until Marinda and Aylin said they had to go back to work. When they left, she remembered that Marinda never answered her question about who she was talking about when she said they all agreed about the rental car.

It was a nice car. Maybe it wouldn't hurt to go look at it.

Grabbing the keys, Demi walked over to the luxury car, opened the door and sat inside. Oh, it was so nice! The seats were leather and soft. The dashboard had all kinds of gadgetry —she could only imagine what they all did. It was so different from the old Jeep Cherokee. Maybe she would look into getting a new car when the Maryland house sold, and she got a job. But she really loved her father's old Jeep. She did have room to keep and park two cars.

Enough time wallowing around, she told herself. It was time to get back to work.

She really wanted to move all those boxes up into the attic today. As she was making her way back to the house, Mrs. Tepen came around from the back of her house. Damn. Guess it was going to take longer to move the boxes.

"Oh, Demi-Lyn. Is everything all right with your car? Did you buy a new one? That is a nice-looking one. Too fancy for me, mind you, but it's nice for someone as young as you."

"Everything is fine with my Jeep, Mrs. Tepen. This is just a rental car until mine is fixed."

"Oh, that's too bad. It is a nice car."

"Yes, it is," she replied. Demi figured the older woman was just winding up. She could only go back inside when the woman was good and ready to let her.

"I have never seen so much activity in this neighborhood at one time. First, it's those men hanging around, and then the girls coming by for a visit. I gave Katia the plate of cookies for you. I hope you enjoyed them during her visit. And isn't it nice that Oliver spent the night?" Mrs. Tepen said with an amused glint in her eye. That little matchmaker. Like she had anything to do with Oliver staying over.

She let the older woman continue talking, nodding at the appropriate times and letting her mind wander. She had a lot to think about—the remaining loose ends to her parent's estate, the lake house and all the boxes, finding a job, Oliver, and now all this crap with someone apparently targeting her, or rather her car, for some unknown reason.

Whoa...wait...back up a minute.

Did Mrs. Tepen say something about men hanging around? "Mrs. Tepen, Mrs. Tepen..." Demi interrupted her mid-sentence.

"Yes, dear."

"Did you say something about men hanging around the neighborhood?"

"Yes, those two men were sitting outside your house yesterday. You know, when Oliver drove you home. They drove off when I came outside again later. You know, when Oliver moved his car back to his driveway and walked back to your house. I went back in, but I like to keep my eye on the neighborhood. They came back and stayed over at the park for a while. They never got out of their car. Just sat right there staring at your house. I have those binoculars, you know; they let me see right into their car. They weren't doing anything other than sitting there. Who goes to the park just to sit in a car to watch a house? Someone up to no good, that's who. So I watched them until another car drove by. I was blinded for a moment by the headlights. You know, the lights are always shining in my windows when cars come around that corner. When I looked again, they drove off."

Demi thanked her neighbor and told her she needed to go. Walking back to her front door, she looked around the neighborhood. She didn't spot anyone out of the ordinary, but would she recognize what or who she was looking for? She hadn't been back at the lake house for years. For all she knew, everyone she encountered was possibly behind the vandalism and the shooting of her tire.

Should she report this? Yes, she should. If it were just the tire, then she'd be able to chalk it up to being an accident. Being in the wrong place at the wrong time. Add in the vandalism of her Jeep at the resort and then the men hanging around watching her house. No, that was too much for her.

Decision made, Demi went back into her house and called Luke. She told him everything that she had learned from Mrs. Tepen, and he promised to look into it. He also mentioned having someone drive by the house a couple of times throughout the night. Just to make sure no one was hanging out at the park or around her house. Demi thanked him, feeling much better about being in the lake house by herself.

Just as she was about to continue working on moving the boxes, she got a call from Simon.

"Hey, Demi. I wanted to talk about the server job and find out what's going on at your home. I heard some men were hanging around watching your house," he said.

"How did you hear?" she asked with a sigh. Damn the Kerrigans and their phone tree.

"Luke texted. He knew Aylin was with Marinda and wondered if I had heard anything about it."

"Figures. Do you Kerrigans ever do anything that the rest of you Kerrigans don't find out?"

Simon laughed before replying, "Nope...not really. You're as good as family, so there won't be a Kerrigan who doesn't know what's going on."

After a few summers in Florida, the Kerrigans realized her friendship with them was more than just for the summer. She texted and talked to Katia and the others constantly, even when she was home in Maryland. So unofficially, they adopted her by the third summer.

"Thank you for the rental car. I appreciate your making sure I have a way to get around."

"No problem. We'll tell you when your Jeep is ready, and someone will bring it to you and take the rental car back."

They continued to talk about the job, with Demi promising to stop by the next day to shadow another server. It would allow her to try out the job and decide if she wanted to take it. Then she'd fill out the hiring paperwork if she decided it was what she wanted to do.

When she hung up with Simon, she finally went back to dragging the last remaining boxes into the attic. Most of them were from her parents' office. Opening the first box on top, she glanced through it and noted it was mostly office supplies. Those would go up into the attic for now, but maybe she'd set up an office in the other room. Eventually. It would be something to think about anyway.

The next two boxes contained books. Demi thought it would be nice to also set up some bookshelves. Maybe Ryleigh would build her some. It would need to wait until she started working or until her parents' house sold, though.

The last box was lighter than the other two. Obviously, it was not full of books. Opening the box, she found it held a couple of journals, a bag of flash drives, and a ledger book. Maybe they were personal journals? The flash drives and the ledger book may be for their business. Picking up one of the journals, Demi thumbed through it and wasn't sure what she was seeing. It wasn't a personal journal. It had some sort of list that made little sense to her.

Oh, well...she really didn't have time to figure it out right now. Maybe she would turn it over to her parents' lawyer. If it belonged to one of the businesses, people, or organizations they worked for, then they may want it back. Their lawyer would return them back to the appropriate people. For now, she'd put it up in the attic with the rest of the boxes and stop to take a break for a late lunch.

Whenever his workload waned, Oliver realized throughout the day that he missed Demi. He wasn't sure if that was a good idea or not. He never thought of Demi in that way growing up, but now that he was, Oliver was all in.

It would be nice having her work in his restaurant. He hoped she took the server position. They really needed her help, and he'd work with her every day. Besides, they could ride to work together since they practically lived next door.

Never mind that keeping an eye on her to make sure she was doing okay after everything that happened to her would set his mind at ease.

And after work maybe they'd go back to either her place or his—she hadn't even seen his house yet—and hang out together, spend some time getting to know each other better.

"Hey, Oliver, I delivered the car to Demi," Marinda said as she walked into his office. His office door was always open in case he was needed to jump in to help in the kitchen. Besides, he liked the noise of the kitchen. It all faded into the background when he was working, like white noise...it soothed him.

"Thanks, Marinda. Did everything seem all right with her?" He didn't want to stick around this morning when Katia showed up, so he wasn't sure how she was feeling with how they had spent the night together. He wondered if Katia had already spilled the beans to Marinda and Ryleigh. It was only a matter of time. They told each other everything.

"She seemed fine. I think Katia said she was going over this morning to check on her. She didn't call me, so I figured everything was good. Aylin and I stayed only long enough to drop off the car."

"Good. Thanks, Marinda."

She gave him a long look, with narrowed eyes. "Something's up with you. I don't have time to figure it out yet, but I will," she accused on her way out of the office.

Shit. When she found out, Marinda was going to go ballistic on him. She'd have the triplets cornering him before long.

A few minutes later, Simon walked into his office. "Hey, just wanted to let you know Marinda delivered the car to Demi."

"Yeah...Marinda stopped by and let me know already."

"Okay. Good. See you later."

Damn it. He couldn't let him leave without making sure he had her working for him. "Hey, wait a minute. Why don't you call Demi about the server job?"

"It's like that, is it?" Simon stared at him, amused. Bloody hell. Oliver seemed to say that to himself a lot lately. He would blame Demi, but it wasn't really anything new for him.

"Just ask her if she wants it, okay."

"I was going to call her about it anyway. I think she'd like...." he paused when his phone beeped. He had a text coming through. Pulling out his cell phone, he looked at it and scowled. "It's Luke. Demi called him about something your neighbor told her."

Oliver was agitated. Luke texted Simon? What the bloody hell! "What was she told? And why is he texting you?"

"Aylin was following Marinda in the car this morning. He wanted to check whether she had mentioned anything. It doesn't seem too bad though. She talked to him on the phone and said something about some men hanging around the neighborhood watching her house."

"Damn it, that can't be good. What's Luke going to do about it?"

"He said he's going to have someone drive by occasionally to make sure no one is hanging around that shouldn't be."

Oliver was a little appeased, but not quite. His first instinct was to leave work and go home to check on her. But he couldn't do that. He was stuck at work because they were about to hit the lunch rush. His crew wouldn't be able to handle the rush, especially since they were down a server.

"Let me know what's going on as soon as you hear anything."

"Don't worry, Oliver. You know we'll take care of her. I'll call her as soon as I'm back at my office. If I find out anything else, I'll let you know."

"Thanks," he said. Sitting alone in his office, admitting he could not help Demi, or find out why all this was happening; it left a heavy pit in his stomach. Shooting off a quick text of his own to Luke to keep him in the loop, he helped in the kitchen before the rush started. He'd do some prep and check the inventory to keep himself busy. He couldn't wait for the day to end. Then he'd find out for himself that Demi was all right.

Over the next couple of hours, Oliver worked through the lunch rush, moving from the kitchen to the dining room and back again. He couldn't wait until Demi took the job. They needed help desperately. Plus, it wouldn't hurt having her around—he enjoyed looking at her—and she calmed him somehow.

Glancing up at the clock, he had only another hour before he could reasonably leave without raising any eyebrows. He'd finish up that paperwork in his office, then call it a day. He was just getting into the paperwork when Marinda stepped back into his office, closing the door.

"Why didn't you tell me earlier you were at Demi's house this morning when Katia came by?"

He didn't think anyone in the family understood the meaning of a private office; himself included. "Hello, Marinda. So nice of you to visit me twice today."

"Don't give me that 'hello, Marinda' crap. Katia said you answered Demi's door this morning half dressed and that on your way out, kissed the hell out of Demi. What gives?"

It looked like the triplet line was rung and info was presented to the hive mind. That took longer than he had expected. "You seem to already know everything, so why are you here asking me?"

"This is Demi. She had a huge crush on you when you were kids. Please tell me you didn't take advantage of that."

Now, wait a minute! How dare she insinuate he took advantage of Demi! "Marinda," he growled at her.

Marinda realized her mistake in accusing him of doing something like that. "I'm sorry, Oliver. I know you wouldn't do anything to hurt her. It's just that she has been through so much, and Katia is worried about her."

That deflated his anger almost immediately. It was so hard to be angry with the girls. They felt deeply and went through their own hell growing up with their mother leaving them at an early age. They were often protective of those they loved. "Look, I'm worried about her, too. I didn't know about her crush on me until recently, but that's not why I'm with her. She's special, and I wouldn't do anything to hurt her, not on purpose, okay?"

"Okay. But be careful with her. I don't know all the details because she talks to Katia more than she talks to me, but she's still dealing with so much since her parents died." She put up her hand before Oliver got another word in. "And I know you understand all about that. You can help her through it all, and I think she can help you, too."

"Yeah, maybe," he said, not wanting to acknowledge even to himself that Demi was the reason for him being so relaxed when she was around lately.

Marinda left his office, but he continued to sit, staring at the paperwork he wasn't completing anytime soon. Could he and Demi help each other work through their grief? He supposed anything was possible.

18

The next day, Demi went to the resort to shadow the other server, Billie. It was exhilarating to her, being able to walk around all day, not having to stand in one spot or sit all the time, getting to talk to a variety of people—some locals, though mostly tourists staying at the resort. It was a great change of pace from what she was used to in Maryland.

Of course, she wasn't really responsible for the tables and their orders yet. It would get way more busy and more hectic as the day went on, but she could handle it. It gave her a purpose and allowed her to feel like she was doing something instead of wallowing in the lake house all day, moving boxes around.

She also liked that Oliver seemed happy to see her and was waiting for her with a smile whenever she came into the kitchen to grab food with Billie. They would smile at each other as if they had a secret.

Billie and the others working in the kitchen and dining room looked at Oliver as though they'd never seen him smile before. She supposed it had probably been a while considering the last year and how he dealt—or rather didn't deal—with the death of his mother. Katia told her in their weekly calls and texts that he wasn't handling it any better than her uncle was, and that he and Simon also had their father getting into everything at the resort to deal with as well. She said Oliver's mood had been foul for the last year and he seemed to withdraw into himself more and more.

So, seeing him smile and looking like he was in a good mood made her happy.

Midway through the morning, Demi finished shadowing Billie when Simon came by and pulled her aside. They walked over to a row of two-seater tables in the corner by the windows, which were not currently occupied.

"What do you think about the job?" Simon asked after they sat down at one of the empty tables.

"I like it. I can see places where it may take me some time to get my bearings, like learning the menu, but the ordering system seems easy enough. And I like the workflow from ordering to the pickup in the kitchen and how the customers either have the meals charged to their rooms or paid at the table," she told him.

"Good. Why don't you come by my office and fill out the paperwork we'll need to get you started?"

"Sounds good. I'm just going to go back into the kitchen and talk to Oliver first, then I'll come to your office."

"I see," Simon said with a smirk.

"What do you see?" she asked, a little miffed.

"Nothing, never mind. If you have any issues with Oliver, let us know, we'll set him straight."

"What do you mean? Why would I have any issues with him?"

"Nothing really. I just remember the mistakes I made with Aylin and how everyone had to step in and put me on the right path. We like you, Demi. You're part of the family with or without Oliver, but it would be nice to see you together."

"Together? Who says we're together?" she asked. Why did everyone assume she and Oliver were a couple all of a sudden?

"Are you saying you're not?"

"Well...maybe? We haven't really talked about it yet." Oliver had come back to her house last night after work and stayed again. She expected him to come back tonight, too. But they hadn't discussed what they were to each other. Were they exclusive? Was he just enjoying sex with her, and someday he'd decide he was done and leave? And she wasn't even going to go into how she felt about him. She'd loved him forever, it seemed. But it wasn't just up to her.

"Okay, well come by my office when you're ready and we'll get the paperwork taken care of." Simon got up from the chair and walked out of the dining room, while she went to the kitchen to find Oliver.

Walking into the kitchen, she didn't find Oliver working with the others at the long steel counters where they prepped meals, nor at the stoves where they cooked them. He must be in his office. Demi walked back there and saw he was working on some paperwork. Should she interrupt his work or come back later after meeting with Simon? She was still so unsure about her relationship with him. Maybe it would be best to come back. Before she could back away from his office doorway, Oliver looked up and smiled.

"Demi, how did it go?" he asked.

She walked into his office and sat down in the chair next to his desk. "It went well. I like the job, and Billie was fun to work with."

"So, are you going to take the job?"

"Yes. I already talked to Simon about it. I'm going over to his office in a minute to fill out the paperwork."

Oliver visibly let out a deep breath, as though he was finally able to breathe again now that he knew she would work at the resort. That made her feel good about her decision.

"Good. Maybe we can drive in to work together sometimes," he suggested.

"Sure, we could do that. No point in both of us driving if we're going to the same place." She wondered if that meant he would continue to stay over at her house at night or if they would meet in the mornings to drive into work.

"Why don't you come over for dinner tonight so we can celebrate your new job? Besides, you haven't seen my house yet."

Demi smiled at him and told him she'd like that before leaving for Simon's office to complete the new hire paperwork. She guessed she would find out her schedule later, but she wouldn't be surprised if Oliver made sure she worked the same hours he did.

Making her way past the lobby, she waved hello to Marinda and Corey, one of the daytime front desk clerks, on her way to Simon's office. When she got there, his door was open, and he was in the middle of his office embracing a woman. She recognized Aylin from when Marinda dropped off the rental car. Not wanting to disturb them, Demi began to slowly back away from the doorway.

"We have company," the woman said when she spotted Demi at the door over Simon's shoulder.

Simon turned, his arm slung around Aylin's shoulders, holding her close to him. "Hey, Demi, come on in."

"Sorry about that. I had to take a break and came down to see if Simon was here," Aylin said uneasily.

"Oh, no! I didn't mean to interrupt you. I can come back later." The last thing she wanted to do was to be responsible for preventing the couple from having some time together.

"Nope, I'm ready to write again."

"And I need you to fill out the paperwork so Oliver will stop complaining to me that he needs another server," Simon added wryly.

Most women might think Oliver only wanted her around to fill the server spot, but Demi knew he wasn't like that. He may want her to work for him so they wouldn't be short-handed, yet he also wanted her there, so he'd be close to her. He wouldn't have asked them to drive into work together if he had only wanted her to fill a position.

Aylin gave Simon a kiss and a quick hug to Demi on her way out. She wasn't sure what to think about that. Demi had never been a touchy-feely type of person, but it was nice that Aylin was comfortable enough to hug her when leaving. Maybe living in Cypress Bay was exactly what she needed right now. She may have lost her family, but it seemed she inherited a larger one just by moving down. It was a nice feeling.

"Before I fill out the paperwork, don't you want to talk to Oliver first since he's in charge of the kitchen and dining area? Make sure I can actually do the job and that he wants me to take it?" Demi really wanted the job. So why was she trying to sabotage it? She knew it was because she was still so unsure about what was happening with Oliver. Was it a good idea to be working with someone she was sleeping with? Probably not. At the same time, she was also looking forward to being able to see him more often.

"No, I had already contacted him before you finished shadowing Billie. The job is yours if you want it."

"I want it."

"Great." He walked around his desk and sat down, picking up a folder with some papers in it. Simon handed it to her. "You can sit over at the table and start on these. I'm going to work on some of my own paperwork while you do that. Let me know if you have any questions."

Demi thanked him, took the folder, and walked over to the small table, sitting in one of the chairs in the corner of his office. She spent the rest of the afternoon filling out paperwork before going home.

19

Oliver couldn't wait until Demi came over to his home that evening. He felt like a kid waiting for Christmas morning after a long night trying to stay awake to catch Santa in the act.

While still at work, he started planning out the evening and what to make her for dinner. He didn't want to make anything overly fancy, but he wanted to impress her. His rissoles topped with prawns and served with potato wedges and green beans would be good. It wasn't the healthiest of meals, but it was quick and easy for him to make and would look like it took longer than it actually did to prepare.

He'd make a quick stop at the store on the way home to pick up whatever he didn't have. He preferred buying fresh food at the farmer's market. They had a great selection of fruits, vegetables, and fresh seafood. But they were only open on the weekends.

Instead, he'd need to make do with the local grocery store chain. They didn't always have what he wanted, and sometimes the quality wasn't great. It would do for tonight, though. And maybe if dinner went well, he'd stop by the farmer's market this weekend and pick up something to cook for her again.

Oliver knew his house was clean because he didn't like clutter and always picked up after himself—at least in the kitchen. He wasn't so sure about the sheets on his bed. He didn't enjoy doing laundry, and his bedsheets were usually the last thing he thought to wash or change. It wasn't like he invited women to his home regularly. Actually, other than family and friends, he'd never invited a woman over to his home. Not that he had been dating lately.

Anyway, changing the sheets was top of his list of things to do when he got home. Along with doing a quick clean-up of his bathroom...and maybe throwing in a load of wash, too.

Figuring he'd better write it all down before he forgot, Oliver made a quick list of what he needed from the store, and what he wanted to remember to do when he got home.

Taking a deep breath and letting it out, Oliver went back to his paperwork. The inventory sheets came in from his managers and team leads, and now he had to go over all of them—decide what to order, then put that order in with the various companies who provided them with food and supplies. He and Simon were looking into a computerized system to automate much of it. It existed, but the resort under the management of their father, John, had never advanced into the current technological age.

It was about time they did.

It would also free up more time for him so he'd be able to spend it in the kitchen instead of doing paperwork. Simon wanted his own paperwork computerized for the same reason. It seemed the paperwork in this place doubled, then tripled itself every time they turned around.

It wasn't what Oliver expected when he came home to take over the kitchen and restaurants. He thought he'd be spending most of his time actually creating food for their guests, maybe putting in some work behind the desk, but not enough that it felt like that was what he'd do all day, every day.

Oliver was scowling over the inventory sheet provided by The Basin team lead. His handwriting was atrocious. How did anyone expect him to order the right things if he couldn't even read what it was they needed? It was another reason to update the inventory and ordering system to a computerized platform.

At the knock at the door, Oliver told whoever it was to come in. Usually he kept the door open, but he couldn't concentrate today. He blamed the bloody paperwork!

The door opened, and Simon walked into his office, sitting down in the chair across from him. He looked exactly how he usually looked. His hair was neatly styled, his clothes immaculately pressed, without a wrinkle in sight. But it was his eyes that told Oliver that his brother was having just as rough a day as he was with the paperwork that wouldn't seem to end.

"Demi finished up all the paperwork. She's now officially hired and ready to work in the dining room," Simon said.

And there it was. Demi may have been the one to fill out the paperwork, but then Simon had to process it. It wasn't as though they had a separate HR department taking care of these things. Then again, maybe they should have one. But that was a discussion for another day. The resort not only belonged to Simon and Oliver, but to their cousins, too. Any large changes needed to be discussed together.

"Okay. Thanks. I'll have Lindsay put her on the schedule. Did she say when she could start?" he asked.

"As soon as you can get her on the schedule, I suppose. Maybe you should talk to Demi about that," Simon said, looking at him a little too long.

Simon had a point.

It wasn't as though he would not see her tonight. He'd ask her then if she could start the next day. Demi could come in with him tomorrow morning and work through the early afternoon shift.

But then how would she get home? He often stayed later

doing paperwork or jumping in to help prepare food for the dinner crowd. He'd need to think about how to mesh their schedules so they could drive to and from work together. She wouldn't be working the long hours he usually worked.

Maybe she'd drive in with him, then go home with Marinda or someone else at the resort. Though he was the only one who lived on the same side of the lake as her. It was something to consider.

"I'll ask her tonight," he muttered to himself, still trying to figure out the logistics in his head.

"What are you doing, Oliver?" Simon asked with a sigh, interrupting his thoughts.

"That's between me and Demi. The last thing I need is someone else thinking I'm not good enough for her." If one more person insinuated his being with Demi wasn't right, he'd hit something.

"I never said you weren't good enough for her. I just want you to think about whether you're ready for her. I know you wouldn't hurt Demi on purpose, but if you're not ready for a relationship, you'll hurt her."

"I will not hurt her. Besides, we're not in a relationship." A relationship? Was that what they were doing? Another thing to think about. He should talk to her and find out where her thinking was on that. He enjoyed spending time with Demi, but he wasn't sure he was ready for a relationship. If they were seeing each other, sleeping together occasionally, that didn't mean they were in a relationship. They would keep it simple. He'd talk to her tonight. Clear everything up.

Just because he thought he could be in love with her didn't mean they had to be in a relationship. The thought made him shudder inside. He was too busy to put in the time needed to make the woman he was in a relationship with happy.

But they practically lived next door, would work together— somewhat—and possibly drive to and from work together. If anything, they would see each other every day. So maybe they were in a relationship. Or at least the start of one. He certainly wanted her in his bed.

And he knew how that sounded. It wasn't like he only wanted her if he could have sex with her. Oliver liked Demi... maybe even loved her. But he wasn't so sure it would work out for them or not. Or if she even wanted him for more than sex.

"If that's what you think, then you're mistaken. Don't make the same mistakes I did with Aylin," Simon warned as he got up to leave Oliver's office.

Bloody hell! He hated when his brother was right. Looked like he really did need to talk to her tonight. They had a lot to clear up.

20

Putting on the finishing touches to her makeup, Demi looked at herself in the mirror. This would do. She wasn't usually a slob, but she rarely dressed up either. Oliver said they were going to celebrate her taking the job. So she thought dressing up a little, making a little more of an effort, would be fun. That's all it was...fun. She wasn't ready for anything else. The royal-blue wrap dress was fun and flirty. That's all she wanted—to flirt and have some fun.

Satisfied with how she looked, Demi sat on the edge of her bed and put on some low black heels. She had little in the way of jewelry, but she grabbed her mother's rosary beads and stuck them in her small black purse. Even if she was only going next door, Demi felt better having them on her. As if a piece of her mother was always with her.

She grabbed her keys from the side table next to the front door and stepped out, locking it behind her, then walked down the street to Oliver's house. Thankfully, Mrs. Tepen wasn't hanging out wanting to talk. The last thing she wanted was to answer questions about why she was all dressed up and if they were going somewhere special.

She knocked on the door and took in the exterior of his house. She realized he had done quite a bit of updating to it. Demi remembered this house looked like a plain white box with a black roof. The people who owned it were an older couple, who, if she remembered correctly, were older than Mrs. Tepen when she was a kid.

Now the home had a large, covered front porch that looked to wrap around the side of the home. The home itself was covered in wood planks, some stained a natural wood color, while others were white. Its roof was still black, but extended on various levels to give it more depth. The front made the home look small, but she knew it would go back toward the lake, like hers did.

When Oliver opened the door, Demi was glad she had dressed up. He stood in the doorway, his eyes roaming over her from head to toe and back up again.

"Are you going to let me in? It's a little cold out here."

"Of course, come in. Sorry," Oliver took her hand and drew her into his house.

The interior just inside the door was rather small, a tiny foyer with a couple of doors. One to the right was open to a small bathroom, while the one on the left was probably a closet, but Demi wasn't about to open it to check.

Oliver led her straight down the short hall where it opened up into a great room comprising of the living room, kitchen and dining room. The entire back wall was filled with windows, showcasing the larger portion of the covered porch, the lake, and a dock beyond the small yard. Columns of wood bisected the area from a hallway leading to a bedroom, another bathroom, and an open office space on the right. On the other side was another door. She thought it must lead into the master bedroom.

"Wow! Your place is wonderful."

"Thanks. We put a lot of work into it to make it look like

this, but it was worth it. Especially the kitchen," he said, directing her to the wonderful smells coming from it. "Dinner will be ready in a moment. Would you like a drink?"

"Sure."

Oliver walked into the kitchen and picked up a bottle of wine he had sitting on the counter, pouring some into the wine glasses he had set out beside it. Once he handed it to her, she took a sip, inspecting the interior of the open space in front of her.

The kitchen wasn't what she expected. Oh, it had the expected high-end appliances. The stovetop looked like something that should be in Oliver's commercial kitchen at the resort. It had six burners and what looked like a grill in between them. He had two built-in wall ovens...no microwave in sight.

A huge double-door refrigerator and freezer with a wine cooler just as tall built in right next to it. She didn't notice a dishwasher, but expected it was on the other side of the island next to the deep sink. The rest of the kitchen was decorated in soft whites and grays, with open wooden shelves around the windows. For some reason, she thought Oliver would have a stark black and white kitchen. Instead, it was light and airy.

Next to the kitchen was a long table with chairs in a light wood. It looked like it would fit most of his family all at once. She wondered if he often had them all come over for a meal. Demi pictured Oliver trying out new foods on his family before putting it on the menu at the resort.

Past the dining room was the family room. He had a large couch and a couple of recliners on either side, all facing a large television hanging on the wall. A square wooden coffee table sat in the middle of the room. The cabinet sitting under the television was long and narrow, the open shelves filled with all types of electronic equipment. That was more of what she was expecting for a single guy living alone.

The timer buzzed, bringing her out of her musings. Oliver went over to one of the ovens and pulled out the most delicious looking and smelling food. He placed it on the stove to cool and walked over to her.

"What are we having?" Demi asked as Oliver led her to the table, where he had already set up two place settings.

"We are having my special rissoles with potato wedges and green beans. Let me just plate it up, then we can eat."

Oliver walked back to the kitchen, where he took out a couple of plates and served up their food before carrying them to the table. He set one plate in front of her and the other in the space next to her, where he sat down.

"Dig in."

They ate in silence for the first few minutes—well, mostly in silence. Demi may have moaned a time or two at how the flavors of the food tasted on her tongue. If it also served to drive Oliver crazy, it didn't hurt.

"So what have you been up to since the last time we saw each other?" he asked. Her mind immediately went to the kiss she impulsively planted on him when she was fourteen. She was so embarrassed. But that wasn't what he was asking her about now.

"Well, I finished high school for one," she said dryly, making him laugh.

"I expected that," he said, smiling at her. "What happened after high school? I heard you went to college and graduated, but I don't know what you did afterwards."

"Nothing exciting. I worked basically at one office job after another until I landed at my last job with a small company doing their scheduling for them. I was with them for three years until..." she said, the memories of why she left causing her to stop talking about it.

"Sorry, Demi," Oliver whispered. At her nod, he continued,

"So it sounds like working for the resort will be way more exciting for you," he said sarcastically.

That got a laugh out of her. She didn't laugh as much as she used to, so it was nice when she did. "Exactly. Working at the resort is like coming home. We spent so much time there during our summers here. So what about you? What have you been up to before coming back to the resort?" she asked.

It wasn't as though she didn't already know, but she needed the conversation to be away from her and the little she'd done over her life. He was a successful chef who could have worked at any restaurant. She got a liberal arts degree and pushed papers for a living. Now she was about to be a server in a restaurant. Not nearly as important as a chef.

They spoke a little more about what he'd done since they'd last seen each other while finishing up the meal.

"That was so good, Oliver. Thank you," she said appreciatively as they got up and took their plates to the kitchen, where there was indeed a dishwasher.

"No, thank you for coming over tonight. I don't cook for anyone that often outside of the resort," he said when they finished and walked over to the couch.

"Oh, you don't cook for your family?" she asked as she sat down.

"Not really," he said absently. "What I really want to do right now is have dessert." Oliver eyed her up and down.

"That sounds good." Demi was giving her own looks at Oliver. He looked good enough to lick.

"But," he sighed. "Maybe we should talk first. About what we're doing to make sure we're on the same page."

That sounded ominous. He obviously wanted to make sure she knew he wasn't serious about her. That they were more like friends with benefits or something. She really didn't know if she could handle that with him. What she really wanted with Oliver was forever. She loved him and wanted to spend her life with him. But she also knew she would scare him off if she told him that.

Instead, Demi would play it safe. Have a little fun.

And she'd keep on telling herself that until she believed it.

In the meantime, Demi would take control of the conversation and keep herself from being hurt when he told her all he wanted with her was a fling or something. Instead, she'd be the one to suggest it. It would kill her inside, but she'd take whatever she could get from him. Then worry about her heart later.

"Good idea. I don't want a relationship. I have too much going on. So we can just have fun, right?" she quickly spat out, hoping she wouldn't choke on the words.

If the conversation weren't wreaking havoc with her heart, she'd laugh at his expression. His eyes widened, and his mouth momentarily hung open before closing. But it quickly changed...desire filled his eyes, and he leaned toward her, leaving her breathless.

"Okay. Since we have that all cleared up, let's move onto dessert," he said, devouring her with his eyes—right before he devoured her with his body.

21

A couple of weeks later, Katia decided they all needed a girls' night. Demi cautiously agreed to let her best friend take over her house and invite all the girls over for the night. Spending the day getting ready for them, she cleaned the kitchen and living room, scrubbing every surface, vacuuming the area rugs, sweeping the floors, and polishing the tables.

She even cleaned the windows, as though they would care about looking out of them during the night. Demi couldn't even view the lake at night unless she had the dock lights on. Even then, it was more of an outline of the dock and a bit of a reflection on the surrounding water.

Demi was feeling a little nervous because she hadn't spent a lot of time with the others...even when she was a kid. Of course, she hung around the Kerrigan triplets a bunch, but she was always closer friends with Katia than Marinda and Ryleigh. Demi spent some time with Hailee, but Hailee often spent more time alone than hanging out with her cousins. And she really didn't know Aylin Miller or Emma Cooper all that much.

Aylin was new to Cypress Bay and hadn't been here when she was vacationing here as a kid. Sure, she'd since met her a couple of times, but the first was a quick visit as Marinda dropped off a rental car for her. The second time, Demi walked in on her and Simon having a private moment in his office. Not conducive to being considered a friendship.

Emma was around, but she was more friends with Ryleigh, going off on their own to make trouble, or that was what Katia always said. Emma and her brother hung out at the resort all the time. Her brother, Sean, was friends with the twins, Luke and Noah.

Demi admitted she was looking forward to getting to know them better now that she had moved there permanently. But she was also nervous about whether she would fit in with them.

Later that night, she was busy pacing the living room waiting for Katia to show up. Her nerves were firing so much that she felt like she was going to be sick. She needed her friend to show up to calm her down and to have someone she was comfortable with before the others showed up at her door. When the doorbell rang, it startled Demi, making her jump a foot off the floor, it seemed. It's okay. Now with Katia there, she'd be fine.

Opening the door, Katia breezed in, carrying a large quilted bag in one hand and a couple of grocery bags in the other. Taking the grocery bag from her, Demi and Katia went into the kitchen.

"I'm so glad you're here. What did you bring?"

"I brought my large slow cooker with shredded Mexican chicken to make the burrito bowls. My smaller slow cooker with the spinach artichoke dip and the rest of the stuff are out in my car."

"Mmmm...that sounds delicious. I'll help you get the rest."

They made several more trips to bring in everything Katia brought with her. It was too much, but when Demi said so, Katia just said they needed the food to soak up all the alcohol

Ryleigh was bringing. Apparently, her sister made a killer margarita.

By the time they got everything in and set up, the other girls were making their way to Demi's house. Marinda was the first to show up, quickly followed by Ryleigh and Emma. Ryleigh got right into making her margaritas in the blender, saying they would need them as soon as everyone showed up.

Aylin was the next to show up. She said Simon dropped her off on his way to Oliver's. Apparently, since the girls were having a night out, the guys decided they would, too. Demi wasn't sure why they chose Oliver's house to hang out, but she figured Simon had something to say about it. He seemed like the type who would want to be close to Aylin.

When Hailee showed up, Ryleigh declared it margarita time.

Not wanting to drink on empty stomachs, they all set about creating their chicken burrito bowls and scooping up the dip onto plates along with other side dishes. Having taken a couple of trips, the girls set themselves up around the living room. Earlier, Demi and Katia had brought in more chairs and side tables for everyone to sit and eat together.

"Okay. It's time to dish about our lives," Ryleigh said gleefully.

Demi wasn't sure about this. She had never had girlfriends in Maryland, where they sat around talking about their lives and what was happening in them. She wanted to be like Hailee right now, who was sinking into her chair trying to make herself as small as possible not to be the first one chosen. Stuffing a tortilla chip filled with dip into her mouth, she occupied herself with chewing.

"I think since we're at Demi's house, she gets to go first. What's up with you and Oliver?" Katia asked, totally throwing her under the bus. What kind of friend was that?

"Ummm..." she started with her mouth half full. "There's not really anything to say."

"Oh, come on! We've all seen the looks you two throw each other at the resort when you're working." Marinda threw in. Great...now she was outnumbered.

"It's not like that. We're just having some fun, but we're not a couple or anything." She didn't want to talk about this. Over the last couple of weeks, she and Oliver had spent almost every night together. She was getting used to having him around at work and at home, either hers or his. It didn't matter to her. She was comfortable in either home. What she wouldn't admit to the girls was that she was in deep. She loved Oliver so much and knew as soon as he decided he wanted out she was going to be devastated.

The girls—except Hailee, who seemed to support her—looked at Demi with a mixture of disbelief and pity.

"Oh, you poor girl. You are totally in denial. Oliver has it so bad for you, and you have it just as bad for him. But we'll let it go for now." Ryleigh mocked.

The talk turned to the triplets and what they had been doing in their lives, jobs, and businesses. They didn't have men to talk about, so they skirted around any men they had in their lives. Lucky for them.

Aylin asked Hailee a question about her book and tea shop, Leaf & Leaves. That was when Hailee was the most talkative of the night. Aylin reached over to grab the pitcher of margaritas to pour more into her glass when Ryleigh gave a high-pitched squeal.

"What is that, Aylin?" she asked.

"What is what, Ryleigh?" Aylin nonchalantly replied.

"That ring next to your engagement ring. Don't play dumb with us. Did you and Simon get married?"

The girls all looked down at Aylin's left hand and noticed the other ring at the same time.

"You got married?"

"What the hell! You didn't tell us?"

"When did that happen?"

Aylin calmed them down before explaining why they got married, telling no one. "We just couldn't wait anymore. Not that we didn't want everyone to be there, but it really was a spur-of-the-moment thing. We were walking downtown after lunch last week and were about to pass by the courthouse. Simon kind of sprung it on me by saying we should just go in and get married. So we did."

"You got married last week and still didn't tell us," Hailee quietly said from her corner.

Demi could tell from Aylin's downcast eyes that she was feeling guilty. She was fiddling with the rings on her finger before looking up at Hailee and then moving her gaze over all of them.

"We were just coming to terms with it ourselves. We're not spontaneous. You all know that. We decided to tell you all tonight since everyone would be together. I didn't even tell Angeline or my parents until right before we left to come here."

The other girls looked appeased by this. Angeline was Aylin's best friend and editor up in Pennsylvania. They were practically attached at the hip. For Aylin not to tell her best friend or her parents about the marriage, then the spontaneity was something both she and Simon were struggling with.

"Do you regret getting married so quickly?" Emma asked.

"Oh no! Not at all! We were a bit surprised with ourselves by getting married so quickly, but it was more that we made an instant decision like that without thinking it to death that surprised us the most. I love Simon with everything I have and don't regret any part of marrying him."

Demi thought about what it would take to love someone so much that they'd marry each other without thinking or talking about it first.

She loved Oliver. For most of her life, it seemed. Though how she loved him now was very different from the childish love she felt for him as a kid. Would she marry him as hastily as Aylin and Simon did? She wasn't so sure.

Her parents loved each other so much, but it took them years to get together. Granted their situation differed from hers and Oliver's, yet really not all that much different if she thought about it. Her parents met and then didn't see each other for a while until her father tracked down her mother and asked her to marry him. But they were apart until her mother got the papers needed to move with him out of the Philippines.

She and Oliver hadn't seen each other in twelve years, then came together almost immediately once they saw each other again. Oliver didn't seek her out though, wanting to marry her. They sort of fell into a relationship, if spending almost every day together at work and then every night together in each other's beds was a relationship.

As the conversations of the girls continued around her, Demi wondered what it would be like to marry Oliver and have a life with him in one house. No trying to figure out who was going where. No sneaking over extra clothes for the next day so Mrs. Tepen didn't start asking questions. They would combine everything they owned into one house and live together.

She envisioned them living at Oliver's house. The furniture she had here wouldn't fit well with what he had, but some of her art and other collectibles would fit in, making the place appear even more alive than it already did. Their home would feel like them, a place for their friends and family to gather— good food and good company.

But Demi knew it for only a dream. There would be no combining of homes with Oliver. They weren't in that kind of relationship. They were just having some fun until one or both of them decided it was enough.

Why did that make Demi feel so empty?

22

With Demi and the girls hanging out over at her house for the night, Oliver invited Simon and Simon's best friend, Joel, over to watch the hockey game. The Tampa Bay Lightning were playing against their rivals, the Florida Panthers. There had been so many fights between the two teams over the years that it was almost as good as watching a boxing match.

He invited Noah, Luke, and Sean over to watch, too, but they couldn't make it. Noah had surgery scheduled at the hospital in Pine Grove. Luke said he had to work. There were some things he had to look into, so he didn't have time to hang out. Or so he said. Sean was in the midst of his latest painting. Though with him, it could be he was in the midst of his latest muse. Sean was a bit of a player, and he never seemed to date the same woman twice.

Other than greeting each other when they first arrived, Oliver, Simon, and Joel really didn't talk much, preferring to eat the subs, chips, and dip Oliver made while watching the game. Every once in a while, they would yell at the television. But only every once in a while.

The first intermission broke them up, with Joel wandering

off to the bathroom. Simon and Oliver went into the kitchen to replenish the food and drinks. When they were done, they all settled back into the living room to talk while they waited for the second period to start.

This was what Oliver had been missing. Hanging out with his family and friends. They were all so busy that they rarely visited anymore—which explained the absence of Noah, Luke, and Sean.

"Aylin and I got married last week," Simon blurted out before shoving a chip covered in homemade dip into his mouth.

Oliver and Joel were in the middle of lifting their own chips full of dip when they were stopped by Simon's proclamation.

"What?" Joel asked, stunned.

"You got married?" Oliver questioned, staring at Simon suspiciously, finally noticing the ring on his finger.

"Yep. We decided one day on the way back from lunch to stop at the courthouse and get married. Figured this would be a good time to let everyone know."

"But you don't do anything without thinking about it forever first," Joel pointed out.

It was true. Simon was not a spontaneous type of guy. Aylin was a little more spontaneous than Simon, which was a good thing for him, but not to the point of suddenly getting married.

"Does Dad know?"

"He does now. I called him before we left the apartment. And after Aylin called Angeline and her parents. The call with Angeline didn't go well at first," he said wryly.

"I wonder why. Did you think no one would care that you both just got married without telling anyone?" Oliver was getting heated up over this.

Simon and their father were the only members of their immediate family left. Sure, they had a ton of cousins, aunts, and uncles, but Simon, Oliver, and their father were their core family.

Since the death of their mother, Oliver thought Simon felt like he needed to hold their family together. Now he went and got married without telling anyone. It was as though Simon didn't care about their family anymore.

He knew these thoughts were unreasonable. Simon getting married was about him and Aylin, not the rest of the family. And it didn't change the dynamics of the family either. But Oliver was so upset that he said nothing for an entire week.

"Oliver, it's not that we planned it. It was a spur-of-the-moment thing. As for not telling anyone...at first, we were a bit in shock ourselves. Once we settled in, we planned on when to tell everyone and figured tonight would be best because everyone would be together."

That mollified Oliver a little. He still didn't like that his brother got married and said nothing about it, but ultimately it wasn't his life and nothing really changed. Aylin was already living with Simon and part of his life and the family. Now it was just official.

"Okay. I get it. And for the record, I'm happy for you and Aylin," he said, admitting that marrying Aylin was good for his brother.

Joel and Simon seemed to let out a breath of relief at Oliver's words. His temper often got out of control quickly, but he was working on it. Actually, other than when he thought about what had been happening to Demi lately, Oliver couldn't think of a time recently when he had let his emotions become all bottled up until they exploded.

It was all because of the time he was spending with Demi. She calmed him like no one else.

The game restarted, and the three got caught up in the action once more. Yelling at the television as if the players could actually hear their taunts and directions. At the next intermission, they all sat back as if needing to recover from their exertion.

"So, Joel...what's up with all the trips you've been taking lately? Having fun without me?" Simon asked with a smirk.

Joel had unexpectedly gone out of town for a while during the time Simon and Aylin were dealing with her stalker. Usually, he was a homebody like the rest of them. Joel and Simon once traveled everywhere together, but as they got older and gained more responsibility—Simon with the resort and Joel with his boats—traveling didn't seem to be something they did much of anymore.

"Things are fine. I just needed to go on a quick trip to take care of some things for my mother," Joel said.

"Anything we can help with? That's a lot of trips to take for your mother," Simon said, his eyes narrowing as he stared at his friend.

"Nah...I'm good."

Oliver thought it was strange, just as Simon thought. Joel's mother, Becca Roberson, was a single mother after Joel's father, Adam Madris, left her when she told him she was pregnant. His mother was amazing, and Oliver always enjoyed following along after Simon and Joel as a kid to her house. As far as he knew though, his father was never seen again. And he couldn't imagine what Joel would need to do for his mother out of town. Ms. Roberson was truly entrenched in the local community. She ran a small farm and sold her fruits, vegetables, honey, and plants at the local farmer's market.

Simon and Joel shared a long, intense look, but then quickly changed the subject. Obviously, something was going on that Oliver was not aware of. They had a much closer relationship. Oliver was more like the tag-along little brother who liked to cause trouble when they wanted to go do their own thing. Today, the friendship lines were a little shorter, and they all—Oliver, Simon, Joel, Noah, Luke, and Sean—hung out together as a larger friend group.

"Did you tell the others?" Oliver asked after thinking about the rest of their group.

"What?" Joel asked in return. It was then that Oliver realized he'd gotten off topic, and they thought he was talking to Joel about whatever was going on with him. He still had no clue after Joel and Simon's cryptic conversation.

"I meant...Simon, did you tell Noah, Luke, and Sean about getting married?" he asked, rephrasing the question.

"I'll tell them later," Simon answered, seeming unconcerned.

Oliver mentally shrugged. It wasn't his place to tell his brother what to do. But they both understood how the family operated. If one person knew, then everyone knew. And with the girls being told tonight as well, that meant word would get to the others before Simon could tell them himself. His brother was about to receive some angry phone calls later.

At the start of the third period, Oliver began thinking about Demi. He wondered if she was also thinking about him. What was it about her that had him feeling bereft whenever she wasn't around? Were they in a serious relationship? He always told himself that he didn't want to get serious with anyone. His life was being a chef, running the resort kitchen, creating new menus and recipes, maybe he'd do some traveling to experience different foods. But to have a wife and eventually children? No, that was never for him.

But now there was Demi. Was his whole belief about a wife and family changing? He wasn't working as long as he used to. That was because of the extra time he wanted to spend with Demi. Was he changing his whole life for her, and was that what he really wanted?

He wasn't so sure what it was he really wanted anymore. Maybe he should take some time to think about it. He was getting in too deep with her and changing his whole life for her. It wasn't too much to ask for him to take a step back for a while. Besides, he really should take some more time looking at the new menu. He'd been meaning to do that, yet kept on putting it off.

Decision made, Oliver would let Demi know he needed to be at work earlier in the day and later in the evenings for a while, and she could drive herself to and from work.

That didn't mean he couldn't spend time with her.

He'd still see her at work. And maybe they'd get together on the weekends. He didn't need to spend every night with her. Feeling better about how he would deal with Demi, Oliver's attention filtered back to the game.

23

The drive into work was an odd one for Demi. For the last couple of weeks, she and Oliver had been driving into work together. Now here it was a few days after the girl's night, and it was the third day she had to drive herself to work.

Demi didn't know what was going on with Oliver, but he called her after the girls left and told her he had to go into work early for a while and they wouldn't be able to drive in together.

He had only stayed over for one night with her, too. He told her that, because he was going to work earlier and staying later that he felt better going home. When she said she didn't mind staying over at his house or getting up earlier when he had to leave, he simply said it was for the best if she didn't.

Something was going on with him, and she wanted to know what it was. Even though she loved Oliver, he was flawed in ways that some described as being purposely emotionally detached. He felt too much and often detached himself from his feelings—or so he thought. Instead, it built up inside him until he could no longer contain it. Demi wasn't one to play games and didn't want to be involved with someone who was in a relationship one minute and was standoffish the next.

But she also knew Oliver and how he thought. He most likely got inside his own head. Maybe someone that night said something, and it got him thinking about how deep they were getting. Oliver shied away from deep emotions. Maybe she should try talking to Simon today at work and find out what they talked about that night. If that didn't work, she really didn't know what else to do. She would need to wait Oliver out until he was ready.

Demi let out a deep breath as she pulled into the resort parking lot reserved for employees. Oliver's car was sitting closer to the building. Those spots filled up quickly, so she knew he had come in early as he said he would.

When she first came to the resort, she thought Simon would have reserved parking spots for the owners—namely him, Oliver, Marinda—and while the others in the Kerrigan family didn't work there daily, at least a couple of spots for anyone who showed up. But that wasn't the case.

She asked Simon about it a week after starting work, and he told her he didn't think it was right to have reserved parking spots. It was first come, first served. So the earlier she arrived, the better parking spot she got.

Of course, Simon lived on the property. His car and Aylin's were almost always parked in the same spots. No one seemed to have a problem with it, and most employees treated those spots as reserved for them. Not because they had to, but because they wanted to. One thing she learned was that the Kerrigan family was well-respected at the resort and in the town of Cypress Bay. And she loved that they never took advantage of that respect.

Exiting her Jeep—and thank goodness she had it back now and in better shape than it was before—she closed and locked her door before walking to the employee entrance in the back of the resort. She was already dressed in her uniform of khaki pants and a white polo shirt with the green Tola Dining logo, so she usually just stashed her purse and keys into a locker in the employee dressing room.

Some employees had a change of clothes or waited to change into their work clothes until they got to work. She enjoyed being ready as soon as she arrived. Though she brought a change of clothes today. Since she was meeting Katia for dinner after work, Demi didn't want to wear her work uniform—even if it was only a pair of khakis and a polo shirt.

When she got to the dining room, she immediately clocked in and checked the roster to see which tables the team lead, Lindsay, had assigned her to for the day. With no one sitting at the tables she was to work that day, Demi decided to find Oliver. She found him in his office, deep in paperwork and with his nose practically buried in his laptop.

"Hey," she whispered.

Oliver's head snapped up at the sound of her voice, a smile forming as though seeing her made her day. "Hey, I'm glad to see you. How was your night?"

It was horrible without him in bed with her. How she got so used to him being next to her at night she just didn't know, but now she barely slept without him. "It was fine. How was yours?"

"Good. Good. It was good," he repeated. "I'm sorry for not being able to spend more time with you right now. I've been slacking lately, and I'm really behind on my work."

"You've been slacking lately?" Demi needed more clarification on that statement because, as far as she knew, the only reason he had started 'slacking' lately was to spend more time with her. Not that she asked him to. He made that decision all on his own.

"Ummm, yeah. You know I've been coming in later in the mornings and leaving earlier in the evenings than I was used to. I really need to get back onto my regular schedule to keep up with my work," he said uneasily.

"I see." And she did. He was totally freaking out about their relationship and was now trying to take a step back. As much as it hurt, Demi really didn't have the bandwidth to deal with someone who was being wishy washy. "Well, that's fine then. I'll just stay out of your way and let you get back to work. Maybe I'll see you around sometime."

Demi turned and walked calmly out of his office, ignoring him when he asked her to wait in an exasperated tone. Jerk! He could have been truthful with her and said he didn't want to get involved with her. Instead, he was giving her mixed signals. One moment he was happy to see her, and the next he was making excuses for why he didn't have time for her. Then to blame her for not being able to get his work done. Fine. That was just fine. She would concentrate on her own work and life. She didn't need him.

So why did it hurt so much?

Rubbing a hand over her chest as if she could relieve the pressure and pain building up in her heart, Demi walked through the kitchen back to the dining room to start her shift. She was relieved people were being shown to one of her tables as she walked in.

The rest of the day went by in a blur. She kept herself as busy as possible, ignoring Oliver any time he tried to talk to her throughout the day. Not that he tried too hard.

The jerk.

Demi found things to do when it was slower in the dining room, like volunteering to cart food to The Tavern or bring supplies to The Basin. She even offered to take the trash out to the dumpster—a task they all tried to get out of as much as possible. Anything to stay away from Oliver. She needed time to herself to sort out how she was feeling about him.

Unfortunately, she couldn't do that as long as they were both working in the same place. She'd take some time to really think about what she wanted to do about Oliver in her life once she got home. Demi didn't want to give up on him, but she also couldn't fight against someone who had yet to decide whether he wanted her.

She didn't think that was where he was right now. He was confused, so there was still a chance. The question was whether she wanted to give him that chance when he finally decided that he wanted her in his life.

Of course, she did! Demi reminded herself that this was what Oliver did when he was overwhelmed. Especially when it involved his emotions. He closed himself up tight until they either went away or he had no choice but to deal with them.

So she'd give him the time he needed to figure it all out. But that didn't mean she was going to go around acting as though she were happy about it. Because she wasn't happy at all. Having another taste of Oliver in her life, then having it ripped away once again left her feeling just as out of sorts as he did. No, she needed space of her own. Even if it was the last thing she wanted.

24

Bloody hell! What did he do?

Oliver knew as soon as the words came out of his mouth that they were crap and untrue. He all but accused Demi of being responsible for his not being able to get his work done. And now, she wouldn't talk to him. He didn't blame her.

He was acting like an eejit—as his mother would always say. If she were still alive, he would have gotten an earful from her by now. Because somehow she'd always find out. He and Simon could never get away with anything without their mother finding out about it.

Oliver wished deep down she were still alive to yell at him. Instead, he was resorting to hearing her voice in his head telling him he was an eejit and needed to make it right.

If only it were possible. Demi was doing everything to ignore him. And he didn't blame her one bit. Every time he tried to talk to her today, she'd turn and walk the other way, or tell him she was busy.

She even offered to take the trash out to the dumpster, for crying out loud! No one wanted to do that. The dumpster smelled horrible, and getting even a couple of feet from it was enough to make a person gag. Taking out the trash meant getting even closer to throw it in, and no one wanted to do it.

He wasn't sure what he really wanted with her, but he didn't mean to hurt her either. Oliver may be confused. He may not be sure what he wanted in his life other than what he was currently doing with his career as a chef and working at the family resort. But he also knew what he said to Demi was the last thing he was actually feeling about her.

She wasn't to blame for his being behind in his work. He did that to himself. It was his decision to change his work hours to drive to and from work with her. He was the one who decided he didn't want to spend all day at work to spend his time with Demi instead.

If he was really being honest with himself, what he said to Simon weeks ago was the truth. He loved Demi. But he was also scared of loving her. Oliver's father loved their mother so much, and when she was killed in an accident just over a year ago, he was devastated.

He was too, if he was still being honest. He closed himself in and became even angrier than he usually was when he didn't let his emotions out in a healthy way. Or at least that was what the therapist said when he finally admitted he needed to see someone after his mother's death.

His family didn't know that he had seen someone. He didn't want them to know. But it worked for him. Made him understand he was allowed to grieve his mother's death, be angry even at the person who was driving drunk that night and killed her. Yet holding it in was not a healthy way to deal with those emotions. Instead, he needed to learn to express himself better, and when the emotions got bottled up, he'd use the breathing techniques to help calm himself down.

He could also admit that since Demi had come back into his life, he hadn't felt the need to use what he learned in therapy all that much. She calmed him with just her presence.

She helped him in so many ways, and she didn't even know it. And then he went and practically accused her of ruining his ability to get his work done.

You are an eejit! His mother's voice rang in his head. *Now fix it.*

And he would fix it. He just didn't know how or when. It wouldn't be anytime soon—as long as Demi was giving him the cold shoulder. Eventually, she wouldn't be able to stay away from him. They worked together most of the week, plus she practically lived next door.

Oliver wondered about getting Mrs. Tepen involved in helping him. Now, that was an idea. He'd think about whether he wanted her help later. The woman's ideas were frequently invasive, especially if she thought she was the reason he and Demi got back together. Living next door would become unbearable with her bragging that she helped bring them together after he stuffed it all up.

His next thought was about what his brother was going to say once he got word about what he'd done. And it was only a matter of time before that happened. He'd need to admit to Simon that he did exactly what his brother said he was going to do...stuffed it all up just like he did with Aylin. He'd need to do the groveling he was told to do. It wasn't something he was used to, and Oliver would need to think hard about how he'd go about it.

For now, though, he had orders to help make. Working in the kitchen would help him clear up his head...and maybe he'd think of a way to get Demi to talk to him again.

While Demi and Oliver were at work, Mr. Heaton contacted the men he hired to reacquire what belonged to him and take care of any loose ends while they were at it.

He wasn't happy they hadn't made any progress yet. They needed to stop sitting around watching the place and take some action. If they didn't contact him soon with some new piece of information that satisfied him, they were going to pay dearly with the loss of some limbs or their heads. Whichever. They knew it didn't matter to their boss.

The men couldn't wait any longer. The old woman was a problem, but they'd take care of her if they had to. They weren't afraid of hurting anyone who got in their way. Especially when it was a decision between their heads or someone else's.

With the latest call from Mr. Heaton, the men were getting desperate and needed to find what their boss wanted. Knowing the house was empty, they broke in, not even worried if someone witnessed them going through the front door. This backward small town wouldn't be able to do any worse to them than Mr. Heaton would do if they didn't find his belongings.

The men went through each room, flipping through items throughout the house, throwing anything that didn't have what they were looking for inside. One worked in the living room, while the other looked through the kitchen. When nothing was left unturned, they walked down the hallway into the bathroom and bedrooms, doing the same until they met back up in the hallway.

"Where the hell is she keeping them?"

"I don't know, but it's pissing me off. If we don't find them soon, Mr. Heaton's going to take heads."

"It's got to be here somewhere. We already searched her car and what was in it. The trailer was empty when we looked in it the other day. She had to have moved it inside the house," the man complained as he threw another item in frustration.

"I say we grab the bitch and make her tell us where they are," the other man said.

"Yeah...let's do that. We've searched enough..." the man

stopped, looking up at the attic access door. "Look here. Maybe she put them up in the attic."

The man pulled down the stairs when they saw the old woman from next door standing at the now partially opened front door.

"Hey, I called the police. You aren't going to get away with breaking in here. You shouldn't be here." The old woman tentatively peeked inside the house.

Looking at each other, they realized she didn't know where they were in the house, just that they were inside. If she called the police, they had to leave. But that didn't mean they couldn't make a point first. The nosy woman would pay for interrupting them.

As one, they rushed from the hallway and through the living room toward the front door before she knew they were there. The force of both men running into the woman knocked her down, causing her head to bounce on the concrete ground before going still.

Not wanting to hang around if she really called the cops, the men ran off down the street to their car, while the woman lay on the ground unconscious, bleeding from her head.

25

After a long day at work, Demi headed home. Just thinking about how her day went made her tired and a little heartsick over Oliver. She couldn't bring herself to talk to or look at him all day. He wanted to talk to her and looked so sad, but she couldn't do it. Her heart hurt too much after what he said to her.

As she approached her street, her mind was on Oliver, so Demi didn't notice the car moving quickly from the opposite direction. It careened close to her Jeep, causing her to swerve to avoid contact.

"What the hell!" she screamed out loud, not that the person in the other car heard her. Thankfully, she kept her car on the road, but her heart was beating a million miles an hour.

The shock of another car coming at her and the possibility of it all ending for her had Demi rethinking her stance about how she reacted to Oliver. Shaking from the adrenaline drop, she wanted to pull over to collect herself, but knew she was almost home. She would just sit in her car after she parked to relax a bit before going inside.

Demi pulled up to her house and parked in her driveway,

leaning her head back against the headrest and closing her eyes for a moment to collect herself. Once her heart rate came down to a respectable level and she stopped shaking, Demi gathered up her purse, the bag with her uniform, and got out of her car.

She quickly recognized a couple of things all at once. It was dark. Didn't she put the light on outside for when she got home? She always left a light on in case she left work late or decided to go out after work to run errands. Today, she left work earlier when the sun was still out, but she met with Katia for an early dinner before coming home. Demi didn't worry about staying too late talking with her since she expected the light to be on.

The light certainly wasn't on anymore.

Second, something big was lying in front of her door, and the door to her home was wide open. Demi was about to run back to her car and call for help from the safety of a locked vehicle when she realized the something big lying on the ground was actually a person.

Demi rushed over and realized it was her elderly neighbor, Mrs. Tepen. The woman had blood running down her face, and she wasn't moving. She was scared that her neighbor might be dead. Reaching a hand toward her, she gently placed her fingers on her neck to check for a pulse. Finding a faint pulse, Demi knew she should call for help as soon as possible. It may mean all the difference in Mrs. Tepen's life.

Grabbing the purse she dropped next to her, Demi opened it and reached for her phone. Her hand shook so badly she could barely hold on to it. Before she unlocked her phone, Luke pulled up in his patrol car, lights strobing. Demi ran to him as he was getting out of his car.

"Luke, we need an ambulance," she said in a panic, grabbing onto his arm as she reached him.

"Demi-Lyn, are you okay? What happened?" Luke asked Demi, looking her over to make sure she wasn't hurt.

"It's my neighbor, Mrs. Tepen. I just got home and found her bleeding and unconscious at my door." Demi tried to drag Luke toward the woman, but he was already running to her.

Luke knelt down and checked over the older woman. "Dispatch, I need an ambulance at Demi-Lyn's place." Luke spoke into his radio.

"10-4, Luke. I've got them on the way," the dispatcher replied in her efficient and professional tone.

"Good. And send a deputy this way, Carol," he told the dispatcher. Luke raised his head and looked at Demi. "What happened?"

Demi felt like she was going into shock. She didn't know what to think anymore. Was this connected to what happened to her car...twice? Was someone so upset with her they would do anything, including hurt other people?

She realized Luke was still looking at her, waiting for an answer. "I just got home. I was shaken up because someone almost ran me off the road around the corner. So I was sitting in my car for a while to calm down. When I got out, I noticed it was dark. I left a light on outside because I never know what time I'd actually be getting home. But then I saw something big in the doorway and my door wide open. I was going to go back to my car and call you when I realized it was Mrs. Tepen. Then you showed up."

"Someone tried to run you off the road?"

Oh! Someone tried to run her off the road! Could they have been the ones to break into her home and hurt Mrs. Tepen? Why would they do that? "I-I...yes, a car came around the corner too fast and almost hit me. I had to swerve to move out of the way." What was happening? She didn't understand any of this.

"Stay here with her and wait for the ambulance. I'm going to check out your house and make sure no one else is inside."

Demi nodded. As Luke cautiously walked inside, she knelt

down next to Mrs. Tepen. "It's going to be all right, Mrs. Tepen. Luke's here, and he said an ambulance was coming. They'll help you," she quietly told the woman, stroking the side of her face with one hand, the other holding the woman's hand.

She heard the sirens in the distance wailing closer and closer. Before she knew it, another car screeched to a halt next to Luke's sheriff's vehicle. A door opened, then slammed shut.

"Demi, are you all right? What happened?" Oliver shouted as he ran toward her.

She glanced up at hearing Oliver. Demi felt like she was physically there, but not really there. The ground was hard beneath her, and Mrs. Tepen's hand was soft in her own, but she was just numb all over.

"It's Mrs. Tepen. Someone h-hurt her," she told him.

"The ambulance must be almost here. I heard it as soon as I turned the corner."

Just then the ambulance pulled up, a man and woman jumped out and ran over, relieving her of her duties of watching over her neighbor. Oliver helped her up off the ground. Stepping out of their way, Demi and Oliver walked to the fence line. She wrapped her arms around her waist and watched as the two worked on the woman and prepared her to be loaded into the ambulance.

How did this happen? Someone broke into her house, and Mrs. Tepen got hurt. Demi didn't know how to feel about what was going on. Was she a target? Was someone out there who wanted to hurt her? And how could they have hurt an elderly woman? Mrs. Tepen may be nosy and overly talkative, but she was the sweetest woman Demi had ever met. She didn't deserve to be lying on the hard ground, bleeding and unconscious. This couldn't go on. Luke had to find out who was doing this. He just had to!

And now Oliver was next to her, with an arm around her shoulders, holding her close to him. It was all so confusing. For a while she thought they were getting closer, like they might actually be in a relationship. Then he stepped away from her, giving her excuses why he couldn't spend the night or drive to and from work together. After what he said this morning...well, she didn't want to think about that. Now here he was, as if he were concerned and cared for her. She just didn't know what to think anymore.

This morning, Demi thought she'd just wait him out. She'd be sad at not being around him as much, but decided he'd figure it out, eventually. Then she had dinner with Katia, and they talked about what was going on with Oliver.

Katia was understandably upset on her behalf. Oliver may be her cousin, but she said he was wrong and that Demi shouldn't wait around for him to get his act together. She'd talked about introducing her to some guys who worked for her and even tried to fix her up on a blind date with one of them.

Demi nixed that idea right away. There was no way she was going to jump into dating other men just because he was taking his time figuring things out. Besides, if it hadn't been Oliver, she wouldn't have been ready to date so soon after dealing with the death of her parents. It was because it was Oliver—someone she had known almost her entire life—that made even thinking about dating right now plausible.

Then that got her thinking about whether this was the right time to date even Oliver. Maybe it was a good thing he was playing hot and cold. She had so much to deal with emotionally herself, and now this happened.

But now he had her wrapped in his arms, giving her strength when she thought she had no more left to give herself. She was so numb that she was willing to let it go, let him take charge. First though, before she totally let herself go, she needed to make sure Mrs. Tepen was being taken care of, then she'd figure out what was done to her home.

26

Oliver had just turned onto his street and saw the activity on the road. When he realized the activity was stopped at Demi's house, his heart almost stopped. The thought that something had happened to her after the big mistake he made earlier in the day made him want to crawl into a hole and never come out. But he couldn't do that. He needed to make sure she was all right.

When he pulled up, he didn't see her at first, but then noticed her kneeling beside a very still Mrs. Tepen. He immediately went over to them to help.

Now they were standing off to the side watching the paramedics take care of Mrs. Tepen, preparing to move her to the stretcher before taking her to the hospital.

Oliver looked down at Demi standing next to him. She had her arms wrapped around herself and stood staring at their neighbor. He thought she might be in shock, and he wondered if he should ask the paramedics to look at her, too. Before he could ask, Luke came out of her house and walked over to them.

"No one is in the house, but it's a mess. Someone really went through everything in it, throwing things around. I'm sorry, Demi-Lyn. We'll find out who did this and make sure you're safe. Damn it! I should have had someone watching you after they shot at your car and then vandalized it," Luke ran his hand through his hair and then down his face in frustration.

"It's not your fault, Luke. How could we have known someone would do this? We don't even know why anyone would want to do these things to my car and home," she reassured him, her voice strained.

"What did happen?" Oliver asked.

"I came home and realized the light I had left on was off, then I saw Mrs. Tepen lying on the ground next to my open door. I was going to call Luke, but then he showed up. How did you know to come here?" Demi asked Luke.

"Dispatch got a call from Mrs. Tepen about a break-in. I recognized your address, so I took the call. But what I really want to know about is the car that almost ran you off the road."

"What! Who tried to run you off the road?" Oliver inquired.

"I don't know. It happened so fast. I was driving home, and as I approached the turn, a car came around the corner almost hitting me. I swerved to move out of the way, and they kept driving. Then I came here, sat in my car for a bit and then you know the rest."

"Do you remember anything about the car? Anything," Luke said.

"Umm...it was a dark car. They didn't have their lights on, but mine reflected off it, and it looked to be large and dark. Kind of like..." she trailed off.

"Kind of like what?" Luke asked.

"Kind of like the car Mrs. Tepen said was sitting at the park watching my house."

"Bloody hell!" Oliver exclaimed. "Something needs to be done, Luke."

"Yeah...I got that, Oliver." Luke replied, glaring at him.

Two deputy cars pulled up at the same time the paramedics were loading Mrs. Tepen into the ambulance. Luke called out to the deputies, telling one to follow the ambulance and keep an eye on the woman.

"If she wakes up, take her statement." The deputy nodded at him and went back to his car to follow the ambulance.

"Pedro, I need you posted outside the house until we can call in forensics," Luke told the other deputy. "This is fucked up. I wish we had our own, so we didn't need to wait on another county."

The deputy walked over to the front door and stood guard.

Oliver knew that the county they lived in didn't have many resources for things like this, but Luke had mentioned in the past that he had a good relationship with the other counties nearby and they frequently helped each other out.

Still, he'd never seen his cousin this worked up before. He wondered if this was how it was when Luke was in the military. The man had been in a unit that deployed often, and he always seemed so tense whenever he came home. And secretive. But he rarely looked like he was one moment away from blowing up at everyone around him.

"I want to go inside," Demi said.

"I'm sorry, Demi-Lyn. You can't go inside yet. I need to keep it secure for now. You should be able to go in tomorrow morning. Do you need a place to stay tonight? I can call Katia to come pick you up," Luke replied, his voice softening.

"No, I want to see inside my home first. You can come with me. I won't touch anything, but I just need to see what they did," she implored.

Luke stared at her for so long—Demi staring right back with eyes that pleaded for compliance—that Oliver wasn't sure who would win the standoff. He was a badass former soldier turned sheriff who intimidated others with a look, but apparently he had a soft spot for women.

"Okay, Demi-Lyn. You can go in. But I don't want you touching anything until or unless I say otherwise. Not that it probably matters since your prints are everywhere. Oliver, you should go in, too. Your prints are probably already inside too, aren't they? No touching anything though. Hear me? I still need someone to come in and take pictures to document the scene, and that means I need to have everything right where it currently is, even if it doesn't belong. Got it?" Luke admonished.

Demi nodded her head and agreed. Oliver wasn't sure she should go into her house and see the damage tonight, but he also couldn't stop her any more than Luke. The woman was determined to find out what happened to her home, even if it meant seeing it would break her.

Not that he thought much would break Demi. She was one of the strongest women he knew. With everything she'd been going through lately, anyone who wasn't strong enough would have broken a long time ago.

Squaring her shoulders back, she lifted her head as though gathering her strength to step into her home and the damage. Together, they walked to the house, ready to step inside.

The house was worse than Oliver had imagined. It looked like a tornado had come through the place with everything thrown all around. Either that or a hoarder lived in the home with stuff thrown around in no particular order.

This was not how Demi lived. Sure, she had a lot of extra stuff since moving in with the boxes full of her parent's belongings from their Maryland home, along with her own items she brought from her old apartment. But those things were mostly still in boxes that had been stored up in the attic.

What he saw now was basically everything that was already out and displayed thrown around the home. Every room was destroyed, and they would have a hard time finding anything worth saving.

Demi carefully walked through ahead of him. Her whole

body was stiff as though trying to keep herself together as they walked through her home. Oliver was so proud of her, though she might fall apart later.

Even those who were strong could only take so much. And he'd be with her to help for as long as she needed.

27

Stepping through the door, Demi gasped at what she saw. The entire home looked like a war zone. Not a single thing inside was untouched, with items littering every inch of the floor. A small path was left through the living room and down the hall. Demi, Oliver, and Luke slowly walked through her house together, stepping over any debris in their path.

Demi's stomach churned, as though the dinner she had eaten that night was going to come up at any moment. Looking around, she saw that the couch was flipped over, as were the side tables. The lamps on them smashed into pieces. Moving into the kitchen, Demi saw that all the cabinets had been emptied, with most of her plates and glasses broken on the counter and floor. The cabinet drawers were all pulled out— also lying on the floor—and the cabinet doors opened with everything strewn all over.

She had to remind herself that this was just stuff. But it was hard. Everything in the lake home was a link to her parents and the summers they'd spent together in Cypress Bay. And now it was all gone. Tears gathered in her eyes without falling. Oliver and Luke stood in place looking around, and then at her with a sense of sadness for her.

She had to see the rest of the house. Walking down the hallway to the bedrooms, she looked up and realized the attic staircase was pulled part of the way down. Her heart skipped a beat at the thought of them getting into what she had stored up there. The boxes she brought down with her from her parents' Maryland home held some of her most treasured possessions from them.

"I don't think they went up into the attic, but we can't be sure. We need to wait until after we document everything. We can go up to check tomorrow," Luke told her.

Demi nodded and continued down the hallway. She came to the room she used to stay in during summer vacations. It currently held a twin bed and dresser. Now the mattress was off the frame, half hanging onto it and half on the floor. The dresser drawers all hung open, a couple of them pulled out and scattered across the room, linens stored in it littered the floor. She was hoping to turn the room into a combined office/library/workout space, though she couldn't even picture it with everything strewn about.

Moving onto the hall bathroom, it was a lot of the same thing...items scattered all over, the shower curtain and rod ripped from the shower stall. She didn't know if she could take going into her bedroom, where she personalized the room more than the other rooms.

Stalling in the hallway, she was hesitant to continue. "Take your time," Luke said.

Settling herself, she walked into her room—formerly her parents' master bedroom when they vacationed. The space she made as her sanctuary was just as wrecked as the rest of the house. Her clothes and hangers were in piles all over the floor, her nightstand and dresser drawers ripped out and emptied, the mattress the same half on/half off as the bed in the other room.

Demi wasn't even sure how she'd go through the room to check out the master bathroom.

Oliver looked over at her, noticing her confusion. "Maybe we can check the bathroom out tomorrow after we clean up."

How could this happen? She knew she kept asking herself this question over and over, but she just couldn't fathom why someone would do something like this. Demi wanted to curl up into a ball and just hide until Luke solved why this was happening and caught the men who seemed to want to make her life miserable.

But she couldn't do that.

She made it through the death of her parents. She made it through the details of going through their estate. She moved to a new town without a job. She could survive this, too!

It didn't hurt that she had the Kerrigans to help her out.

She turned and walked out of the bedroom, down the hall, and out the door of the house, while trying not to look at any of the mess. Once outside, she didn't know where to go or what to do. It was late at night, and the only people around were Luke, Oliver, and the deputy standing guard at her front door. The lights of the patrol cars flashed in the darkness. Several other neighbors had come out of their houses, curious about what had happened in their otherwise quiet neighborhood.

Great! That was just what she wanted. For her neighbors to wonder what she brought to town with her. Turning away from the people watching from porches and the edge of their properties, she looked at Luke and Oliver, unsure what to do or say.

"I'm sorry, Demi-Lyn," Luke said. "I'd like to let you pack up some clothes, but I can't let you touch anything yet. Would you like me to call Katia for you?"

"No, you don't need to call her. My car still works. I can use my car, right?"

"Of course, it's not part of the crime scene."

Crime scene.

How did her life become a series of crime scenes? "I'll just drive over to Katia's myself. You know she always stays up way too late anyway."

"You don't need to call or go anywhere. You're staying with me, Demi," Oliver declared.

Maybe it was the shock of the destruction of her home and finding Mrs. Tepen lying on the ground in front of it, unconscious and bleeding from her head. But she didn't want to argue with anyone about where she'd spend the night.

Honestly, Demi didn't think it was a smart idea to drive anywhere on her own. She was trying to hold herself together, but she seriously wanted to find a place to be alone and fall apart a little.

Oliver may switch back and forth from hot to cold and back again, but telling her she was staying with him was exactly what she needed right now. Demi didn't want to think about what came next or how she'd get to a safe place for the night. Or that she wouldn't have any of her own clothes and toiletries for tomorrow.

No, she was grateful he was taking charge. That both he and Luke had been taking charge. But as soon as she got through this, Demi was taking charge of her life. She didn't want to be a victim anymore. She wanted to be strong and build a life in Cypress Bay, even if events like this or Oliver's hot and cold behavior tried to destroy her.

Still, being grateful didn't mean she wouldn't push back at his highhandedness to show him she couldn't be handled quite so easily.

28

Luke looked at him curiously. "I'm sure she can stay with Katia."

Oliver glared at him before repeating, "She's staying with me."

Luke just lifted his eyebrow at him. His cousin was trying to give Demi options of where to stay, but he was seriously getting pissed off at him for suggesting she stay with Katia.

What did he think he was going to do to her? Everyone by now knew they had been seeing each other, so he didn't understand where all this was coming from. Other than Luke wanting to yank his chain and rile him up. The bloody jerk!

"No, I'm not," Demi replied.

"Yes, you are," Oliver insisted. They stared at each other—or rather, Oliver stared and Demi glared—each wanting their own way.

"Okay, I'm just going to go over there," Luke said, pointing to the front door area of her home. "You let me know if you need anything else."

Oliver watched Luke walk away before turning back toward

Demi to plead his case about why it was better for her to stay with him tonight.

"Demi, please. I know what I said earlier was wrong, and we don't need to talk tonight about how much of an ass I was. I knew I'd made a mistake as soon as I made it, and I'll do all the groveling you need me to do later. But, Demi, I couldn't stand it if you weren't with me right now. I need to know you're safe. I need you in my home with me. I miss having you next to me at night and when I wake up in the morning. I've slept like crap these last few days, and I've been taking it out on everyone around me. Please, come stay with me." Oliver rambled on, hoping his heartfelt speech would convince her to come stay with him.

He truly didn't think he could manage another night without her. Not because he missed making love to her—he did, but that wasn't why he wanted her with him. They'd just sleep, and he would be happy with it. He held his breath, watching the emotions change from anger to confusion to relief on Demi's face as she worked out what to do.

"Okay," she whispered, her shoulders down as if almost in defeat, but more likely in pure exhaustion.

He let out a huge breath of relief at that quiet word. He didn't realize how much it meant to him to have her agree to come stay with him.

Luke walked back over to them to let them know the others would come by later that night to document her home. "Can I have your house keys? I'll make sure your home is locked up before we leave." Demi handed him her house key. "Thanks. I'll bring them back tomorrow. I'll also call in the family to come help you clean up in the morning."

"Come on. Let's grab your purse and bag," Oliver said.

They gathered up her belongings from the ground that she had dropped when she saw Mrs. Tepen lying on the ground, hurt and unconscious. Oliver didn't want to think about how the older woman was doing. She may be a pain in the mornings when he tried to leave for work, always stopping him to talk, but she was also a lonely woman who just wanted some company. Mrs. Tepen was sweet and kind, if a little manipulative when she wanted someone's attention. Still, the last thing he wanted to think about in this moment was whether she would survive the attack on her.

He took Demi's hand before walking toward his house for the night, closing out the activity still going on in and around her home. Oliver found he needed to take care of Demi. She calmed him in a way no one else did, and he hated to see her go through another violent incident.

They moved through his house and straight to his bedroom. Dropping her purse and bag on the chair, he left her by the bed and took out one of his t-shirts from a dresser drawer, then walked to the connecting bathroom and pulled out a new toothbrush and a towel.

Oliver went back to Demi, standing in front of her. "Why don't you take a shower? You can change into my t-shirt and climb into bed. Get some rest. I'll be here if you need me." With a nod, she turned and walked into the bathroom, closing the door behind her.

Walking into his living room, he paced around, angry that their neighbor was hurt. What if it had been Demi? What if she had come home earlier? Or had been home when they broke in? To come home to find her lying on the ground bleeding and unconscious...his heart would have cracked in two. He didn't know what to do about his feelings for her.

Oliver needed to keep her safe.

He felt that what had happened was somehow his fault. If he hadn't pulled away from her, then would she have come home on her own, almost getting run off the road, or worse? He admitted she probably would have. It wasn't like she spent all her time with him. Katia was her best friend down here, and they likely would have had dinner together tonight either way.

But he still thought it could have all been averted if he hadn't been a dumb ass. He had a lot to make up for. But tonight his only concern was making sure Demi was comfortable and slept.

Hearing the bathroom door open, Oliver walked back to the bedroom as Demi got into bed, nestling herself under the covers and closing her eyes. He went to his dresser, pulling out a pair of boxers and a t-shirt. The last thing he wanted her to think was that he was going to bed looking for sex. Of course, he got hard every time he was near her, but he didn't want her to feel uncomfortable while they were sleeping.

Slipping into the bathroom, he quickly got changed and brushed his teeth. When he was finished, Oliver left the bathroom. Demi was restless in bed, making micro movements as though trying to get comfortable. Lifting the edge of the comforter, he slid into bed, spooning himself behind her. He placed one arm under her head and the other around her waist, resting it over her stomach, his hand cradling her between her breasts. She instantly calmed, sighing before her breath evened out and she slid into sleep.

Oliver closed his eyes, satisfied that Demi would be safe, and quickly fell asleep.

"That fucking bitch! If it weren't for the old lady, we would have had what we were after."

"Yeah. It had to be in the attic. There's no other place they could be. Unless she already turned it in. Stupid cops are all over the house now."

"Well, we took care of that meddling neighbor. Hope she's

good and gone. Should have hit her again and made sure it was done."

"It doesn't matter. Even if she wakes up and tells the cops anything, they still won't find us. We'll need to be more careful, though, now that the cops are hanging around. We probably won't be able to go back into the house to search the attic as long as they're watching it. So, we'll need to grab the woman instead. Force her to tell us where it is. While they're looking for her, one of us will go in and grab what we need. Then we can take care of the woman and dump her somewhere before heading home to give the boss his property."

"Well, we'd better figure out how to do all that soon. Mr. Heaton will not wait forever. The last thing we need is him coming down to take care of it himself and us with it."

"Don't worry. She'll screw up and we'll grab her. Easy."

Sitting in the rented cabin across the lake, the men continued to make plans about how they would grab the woman and what they'd do to her once they got her.

Knowing they may not be as safe from the boss's wrath as much as they would think they were, they also talked about what they'd do to stay out of his bad side, and if he wanted more answers, why they didn't have his property yet.

One thing they knew...they were going to make the woman and anyone else who got in their way pay for all the trouble they were going through.

29

She needed to get out!

Demi saw herself walking through her house, knowing the men could get to her at any moment. Why was it taking so long for her to move to the door to close it so they couldn't come in? It seemed as though every step took her further and further away from the door. She paused, hearing a voice on the other side of the front door.

"I know you're in there. Leave now before the cops get here."

Mrs. Tepen.

What was she doing here? Were the men already in her home?

It was too late...she was already in danger. She didn't stop the men from getting into her home. She tried to leave, but the door seemed even further away from her than before.

Hearing footsteps coming quickly from behind her, Demi turned and saw two faceless men running toward her. Panicked, she didn't know what to do. Did she run and hide? But how could she? Every time she tried to move, the distance to where she wanted to go grew more and more.

And they were coming up on her too fast.

Before she knew it, they were brushing past her. She could feel them, but they were gone before she recognized their presence.

A scream sounded from outside.

Mrs. Tepen!

They were hurting her, and she couldn't make it outside to help her. She screamed out for help, but nobody came.

"Demi. Wake up, sweetheart; it's just a bad dream. Demi. Come on...that's it."

Demi heard someone else calling for her, telling her it would be all right. Waking up with a start, she was confused about where she was, still stuck in her nightmare. She was scared that the men were waiting for her.

"Demi, it's all right. I've got you. No one is going to hurt you. You're safe, sweetheart."

Slowly opening her eyes, she saw Oliver looking at her with concern. "Oliver?"

"Yes, that's right. You were having a nightmare, but you're safe. I've got you."

And he did indeed have her. She was wrapped around Oliver, his arms cradling her and holding her close, while she was draped over his body, her head resting on his shoulder.

"Do you want to talk about it?"

"No. No, I'm fine. It was nothing."

His mouth opened, as though he wanted to say more, but she really didn't want to burden him with her bad dreams. "Really, Oliver, I'm good. I just want to go back to sleep."

"Okay. Sleep now. I'm here if you need me." Oliver shifted them so they were facing each other, her head still resting on his shoulder, her legs entwined with his.

Closing her eyes, Demi pretended to fall back asleep. Her mind was racing after the nightmare. In no way could she go back to sleep now. She tried to even out her breathing so Oliver would rest.

Maybe she should leave Cypress Bay. Go back to Maryland. Or somewhere else. She wasn't tied to a location anymore. It wasn't that she couldn't find a new job in a new place.

Sure, she had an advantage coming to Cypress Bay. She had her parents' summer lake house to move into, so she didn't need to find a place to live. She had Katia and the rest of the Kerrigans, too. It would be harder to move to a new town with no place to live and no friends around to help. She honestly didn't know what to do.

A lot of bad things seemed to happen to her recently, and they all appeared to revolve around her being here in Cypress Bay. Plus, she was confused about why Oliver even wanted her in his house and bed. Was it just because he wanted to take care of her? If that were the case, she could have stayed in his guest room.

She was so confused since Oliver kept giving her mixed signals. One minute he wanted her close, the next he was making excuses for not seeing her, and now he was back to wanting her in his life. She just didn't have the bandwidth for this back and forth with him.

Exhaustion finally slowed Demi's overthinking. She was no longer pretending to sleep and was instead fighting to stay awake. She didn't want to go back to sleep and have those dreams again. Telling herself she'd stay awake if she wanted to, Demi fell asleep before she even tried.

"Demi, I came as soon as I could. Luke called early this morning to tell me what happened. I can't believe someone broke into your house and then had the nerve to hurt Mrs. Tepen," Katia said, handing her a bag of clothes.

Katia had shown up at Oliver's house early that morning with some new clothes for Demi to wear, knowing she would need something to wear to clean up her house. Her own clothes would need to be washed and organized.

"Thanks, Katia. I'm so glad you're here. Let me go change real quick and we can walk over."

Taking the bag, she walked into Oliver's bedroom and quickly changed out of the clothes he had given her to wear that night. She really wasn't looking forward to cleaning up her house. Demi remembered what it was like last night and wasn't sure she was ready to see it again.

But she couldn't put it off. Katia showed up to help; Oliver was going over with her for a while until he had to go in to work, and Luke said last night he was going to meet them at the house, too.

When Demi, Oliver, and Katia walked over to her house, Luke was already there with Aylin and Emma. She didn't expect anyone else would show up to help. She was both grateful and embarrassed by the need for help.

"Hey, Demi. We're sorry to hear about what happened to your house and neighbor. When Luke called Simon earlier, I told him I'd come by to help you clean up. I grabbed Emma along the way," Aylin told her, stepping up to her to give her a quick hug.

"Hi, Demi. Just point us to where you want to start and we'll get you back into your home in no time," Emma said, also giving Demi a quick hug.

"I'm not really sure where to start. There isn't a spot that doesn't need to be cleaned up." Demi really was at a loss where she should start cleaning.

"We got everything documented last night, so we're good to clean up," Luke said as he handed Demi her house keys.

She unlocked the door and pocketed the keys. Before opening the door, she asked Luke, "Have you heard anything about Mrs. Tepen?"

"I checked on her earlier. She's awake and resting."

Demi was happy to hear she would be all right. She was

really worried about the older woman and was afraid she wouldn't make it. Mrs. Tepen may be a pest, always wanting to waylay them on their way out the door, but she was a wonderful woman, and Demi admitted that she actually enjoyed talking to the woman. Even if it was sometimes at inconvenient times.

Demi opened the door and almost gasped at the mess. No, wait...that wasn't her. Aylin and Emma gasped behind her at what they saw.

"Oh, my God! Demi, you saw this last night? How could you possibly sleep after seeing this? I would have curled into a ball and cried all night," Aylin was trying to commiserate with her, but what she didn't know was that she hadn't really slept well last night. Of course, seeing it again now, it looked worse in the light of day than it did last night.

"Now I understand why you don't know where to start," Emma added.

"Okay...let's split up," Katia said.

"I want to clean up my bedroom. Can you come with me?" Demi asked Katia.

"Of course."

"Emma and I are going to start on the kitchen. Luke, Oliver, maybe you two can start with the living room before you need to leave for work," Aylin said, taking charge as she split the rest of them up.

Demi and Katia worked their way down the small path through the living room and down the hallway to her bedroom. She stopped at the doorway and peered inside. She couldn't believe the destruction.

Katia stood behind her and lightly rubbed her back. "Don't worry. We'll get everything back to normal for you."

Normal. She didn't really know what was normal anymore. And if that meant her life going back to the way it was, she thought nothing would be normal again.

30

Back at work, Oliver was ruminating over what was going on with Demi. It seemed as though she was pulling away from him after she woke up in the middle of the night. And no, he didn't believe she was fine, or that she fell back to sleep right away after what was definitely a nightmare.

This morning she was walking around as if she were in a trance, moving from one room to another as she cleaned up the mess in her home. Seeing the bags and dark skin under her eyes made her seem fragile. But Demi had a core of steel running through her with how she walked right into her house and got to work.

Marinda stepped into the kitchen as he was plating up a meal for the dining room.

"How's Demi?" she asked.

"She's fine. As far as I know, she's still cleaning up her house with Katia, Aylin, and Emma," he replied.

"She's fine? Oh, you silly man. Is that what she told you, and you believed her?" Marinda taunted.

"Hey, I know '*I'm fine*' is what women say so men will fall into their trap so they can tell us we know nothing, but I'm not going to try to guess how she's feeling when she won't tell me. Of course, she's not fine, Marinda! She came home to find our neighbor hurt on the ground outside her wrecked home. Oh… and that was after the guys who broke into her house and hurt Mrs. Tepen almost ran her off the road!"

"It's not a trap," she said unconvinced. Oliver gave her a disbelieving stare. "Okay, maybe a little one. Look, I am sorry to hear she's having such a hard time right now. I'll stop by after work to check on how she's doing and to see if she needs any more help."

"She'd like that. Demi can handle this, but she needs to know we're there to help her get through it, too."

"Absolutely! We'll rally around her and make sure she knows we're there no matter what." At his nod, Marinda left the kitchen.

Let her try to figure out how Demi's feeling. He could go only by what he saw and what she told him. He wasn't a bloody mind reader. But he admitted it didn't take a mind reader to know Demi wasn't handling everything going on well, or that she was anything but fine.

Maybe it was a good thing that Demi seemed to pull away. He really didn't have the energy to put more on his plate right now.

But then he remembered how he felt when he drove up to the house and saw all the emergency lights flashing and Demi sitting next to an injured woman lying on the ground in front of her house. And the way she looked last night in his bed. And this morning as they started cleaning her house.

No, he couldn't stay away from her. He wouldn't.

If he'd just be honest with himself, he'd admit he was in love with her. That scared him. A lot! What would he do with someone in his life all the time? Maybe he should just play this relationship thing by ear. See what Demi wanted to do and follow her lead. Everyone already knew he didn't have a clue.

So what if he loved her?

Bloody hell...that wasn't supposed to come out. Oliver was going to push that thought right back down. And it could stay there for a long time or at least until he got a hint from Demi that it was time for it to come back out. He was used to holding in his emotions and burying them deep. He'd do it with this too.

Oliver only hoped he wasn't making a mistake. The last thing he needed was Simon telling him, "I told you not to stuff it up." He did not want to be like his brother and mess up his relationship before it even began.

"Oliver, I heard about what happened at Demi's house. How's she doing?"

He looked up from where he was plating the next meal to see his father standing on the other side of the long metal table.

"Hey, Dad. She seemed fine when I left her house this morning. We all went over to help clean up."

"That's good. I couldn't imagine what it must be like to come here after everything she's been through, only to find someone's broken into her home. And after her car was vandalized in the parking lot, too," his father said. "Talk about bad luck."

His father said nothing about the other incident where Demi was shot at as she came into Cypress Bay. Luke was probably keeping that one close, but it was a miracle that news didn't spread further. Especially with their family. Things like this didn't stay secret for long, and it would only be a matter of time before everyone knew. Besides, both Gabe and Logan at the auto shop knew about it, too, since they found the bullet in her tire and called Luke.

As for bad luck, Oliver wasn't so sure it was. There were too many things happening to her specifically ever since she arrived. That couldn't be a coincidence. But he was sure Luke was looking into it.

"Yeah. You know, she'd probably like a visit from you at some point. Maybe not now though, since she's still cleaning up her house. Demi will probably take some time off, but once she's back, stop by and visit her. Just not during the lunch rush," he warned with a smile.

"That's a good idea. It's been a while since I've seen that girl. I heard she took the server job here, but I haven't been able to catch her yet."

Oliver smirked at the thought of his father trying to catch Demi. She was turning out to be a great server...the best one they had, actually. And part of that was because she did ten things at once, never seeming to stop long enough to catch a breath.

"I need to get going. Got a job to do upstairs. See you later, Oliver," his father said.

"Bye, Dad."

Oliver watched his father leave the kitchen. He was happy to see him more relaxed a year after losing Mum. At first, his father created all sorts of chaos at the resort, butting into the other employee's jobs. He really couldn't blame him. Oliver didn't do all that great after losing Mum, either. And Dad had lost not only Mum, but a few years earlier had lost his parents during the pandemic. One loss after another, though Mum was the tipping point that knocked him sideways.

That led him to think about Demi and what he'd do if he ever lost her. Oliver could deal with not being with her if she decided she didn't want to be with him. But he wouldn't do well if she died. He'd end up like his father, trying to kill the pain by getting too involved, to the point he made more of a mess than helped.

Shaking off thoughts of anything happening to Demi to cause her to no longer be with them, Oliver put his attention back on plating up the food. He could do it in his sleep, yet concentrating on the food gave him joy, and he needed some joy in his life more than anything.

31

The sun set behind the trees lining the lake. The soft glow of light faded into darkness before her eyes. Demi took in the last bits of the day as it disappeared through her back window. She wondered what she was doing in her home by herself when she'd rather be with Oliver. After everything that transpired since she came back to Cypress Bay, she was not really feeling safe in her own home anymore—so why did she stay after everyone left?

After Oliver and Luke had to leave for work, Katia, Aylin, and Emma stayed for a while, helping her clean up. Throughout the day, other members of the Kerrigan family also showed up, either to offer support or to help with the cleanup.

Noah came by, though he couldn't stay as he had patients scheduled, saying he wanted to check for himself she was all right.

Hailee and Ryleigh stopped by to help for a bit—with Joel Madris following right behind them—jumping in with removing some bags of trash that were piled up just outside the door. Ryleigh also made note of some of the damage to cabinet doors and drawers in the kitchen, saying she'd be back another time to fix them.

Marinda stopped by after work to check on her, and Simon took out more bags of trash when he picked up Aylin. Even Emma's brother, Sean, showed up with lunch for them midday.

She had never felt more support or love than she did around the Kerrigans and their friends.

They were all gone now. Gone back to their own homes for the night. And here she was, all alone. In an empty house that was just recently broken into, and her neighbor injured on Demi's front stoop.

Oliver came by after work to see if she needed any more help and to ask if she was okay, but then he left and went back to his own house.

Without her.

And she let him leave. Was she supposed to tell him she wanted to stay with him again tonight? Or did he take Demi at her word when she told him she was fine now that her house was back in order?

She was lying.

She was not fine.

She was scared out of her mind and didn't think she wanted to stay in her house by herself anymore.

Maybe she'd call him and ask if he'd come over for the night. Sleeping in her own house would be better if he were by her side.

Dialing his number, Demi waited while it rang twice, then went straight to voicemail. Hmmm...his phone was probably uncharged, or he left it in the other room and didn't hear it. She could just walk over. She didn't need to stay here by herself. Oliver let her stay over last night. If she went over to his house and told him she was not fine, he'd let her stay over again tonight.

But first, she needed to make sure no one was outside waiting for her. The men who broke in hadn't been caught yet. Luke said not to worry. He'd find them. But she was still cautious. They could get to her property—either her Jeep or her home—three times since she came to Cypress Bay. She would not bring that up to Luke though. He was doing everything possible to find out who was doing this, and she didn't want him to feel bad for something that wasn't his fault. He already thought he should know something by now. Demi wasn't sure how he figured that, but that was Luke...always taking on responsibility even when he had no control over it in the first place.

Okay, no one appeared to be outside. Looking over at Oliver's house, she frowned. His car was in the driveway, but all the lights were off. It was as if he had gone to bed already. It kind of made sense since he had to get up early to work the morning shift at the resort. Though it still bothered her. How was he able to go to sleep so easily when her whole life was falling apart?

Demi, his whole life isn't falling apart. Of course, he'd be able to fall right to sleep.

She could call Katia instead. Demi dialed her number, then hung up before the first ring. What was she doing? Sleeping here by herself was no problem. Everything was fine. She'd go to sleep, nothing would happen, then in the morning, she'd get ready and go to work.

Demi hurried down the hallway. She left all the lights in the house on so she had no trouble seeing where she was going. She didn't care if the neighbors thought she was crazy. There was no way she was turning out a single light. She had her outside lights on, too. No one was going to sneak up on her tonight.

Since everyone helped to clean, the house didn't even look like it had been trashed just this morning. Sure, there were fewer items in the house now. Much of it that was broken had to be thrown away. She was down to a couple of plates and glasses. The only lamp in the living room to survive was the metal one her parents had behind a chair. Thank goodness for canned lighting, or the room would be full of weird shadows with only the one light on.

Passing by the guest room and bathroom, those lights were blaring, too. One of the dresser drawers in the guest room was broken, as was one of the cabinet doors in the bathroom. Ryleigh said she would come back later to fix those along with the kitchen damage. Entering her bedroom, it looked like her sanctuary again, though moodier with fewer lights. For a bedroom, that wasn't a bad thing.

She and Katia made sure that this space, more than the others, was restored to the way it was before. They did heaps of laundry to clean out whatever dirt and grime was brought in by the men who broke in.

It was like they had emptied her closet and dresser, throwing all the clothes on the floor and stepping all over them. Luke said it was more like they were looking for something, and the clothes and bedsheets were trampled as they went from one area to the next for whatever they were searching for.

That so didn't make her feel better. Luke looked abashed when she said as much, making his apologies before going back into the living room to help that morning.

Now she was dreading getting into bed by herself to go to sleep.

"I can do this. I don't need anyone with me to sleep in my own house," she said aloud, needing to hear someone talking, even if it was herself.

Besides, except for a few items, the room didn't look any different than it did when she left it yesterday morning to go to work. No problem...she could do this!

Demi changed into her pajamas, placing a pair of pants, a

shirt, and her shoes nearby. She never knew when she would need to get dressed quickly. Next to the clothes was a baseball bat she found in the back of the bedroom closet as they were cleaning. She could also never be too careful and liked knowing something was there for her to use as a weapon if needed. Climbing into bed, she buried herself in the comforter, giving herself some respite from the light she refused to turn off.

She could do this. She could do this.

32

Early the next morning, Oliver was in the kitchen helping the others he employed to do the prep for the day. He really didn't need to be there this early, but he couldn't seem to sleep well last night. He kept thinking about Demi and how she was really doing.

When he stopped by after work yesterday, she seemed a little jumpy and hesitant when he asked her how she was doing and if she needed anything. His gut told him she was not doing well and could use some time away from her house, but he let his brain override what he felt, told her to have a good night and went to his own home.

Alone.

That was the problem. He spent the entire night overthinking what he should have done. He should have asked her if she wanted to come with him to his house. Or stayed the night with her at her house. There was no reason for her to stay by herself when he really wanted her to be with him, and he hoped she really wanted him to be with her.

Oliver almost went over to her house more than a couple of

times during the night, but couldn't make himself actually leave his house.

Then, when he finished overthinking his own actions, he started in with what Demi must be going through on her own overnight. One moment he thought she must be scared out of her mind sleeping in the house on her own, and the next she was the bravest and strongest woman he'd ever met.

She was probably a bit of both, Oliver thought.

Someone who was scared out of her mind after her house was broken into and trashed, and staying in the home by herself, was brave and strong. Since Demi came back to Cypress Bay and Oliver got to know her as an adult, he thought her one of the strongest women he'd ever known. She'd had one obstacle thrown at her after another, and while she broke down a few times, he wasn't one who thought crying was a sign of weakness. It was a sign of strength, which made him the weak link in their relationship.

It took him a long time to cry after his mother's death. He finally did during a therapy session a few months ago, and it made him feel lighter than he had in a long time. But he still had a bad habit of holding in his emotions until they couldn't be contained any longer. He had to work on that.

Deep in thought, with the sounds and tasks occupying his focus, Oliver was surprised when Demi came into the kitchen dressed for work. He thought she would take a couple of more days off and was prepared to call in another server or have to cover some of the work himself.

"You're here," he said incredulously.

"Where else would I be? I don't need to be hiding out just because my home was broken into," she growled at him.

Her tone slightly took Oliver aback. "It's good to see you here and taking it all so well." He would go over and drag her into his office, but he was wrist deep in some dough, kneading it for the bread they would bake later that day.

"Yeah, well, I should get to work. See you later," she said, clocking in, then walking back out of the kitchen into the dining room.

She was on the schedule, so it wasn't as though Demi wasn't supposed to be working, but she was two hours earlier than she was scheduled to start. Maybe she wasn't taking the break-in as well as he thought.

Bloody hell!

He should have stayed with her last night. He was kicking himself now for not going with what he felt and staying. If he was uneasy about the break-in, then she must be even more so. Never mind the fact that their shared neighbor was lying in a hospital bed recovering from her injuries after surprising the men who broke in.

Thankfully, Mrs. Tepen was doing well and should be released soon. Luke said she woke up, but wasn't able to tell them much more than they already had, although they got a better description of the car the men were driving. Mrs. Tepen would stay with her daughter once she could leave the hospital until she was well enough to return to her own house and live on her own again.

He would need to pull Demi into his office once he was done with the dough. If he didn't think she was up for being at work, then he'd send her home, but not on her own. Because obviously she wasn't comfortable if she was here so early. Maybe he'd call one of the girls. Maybe hanging out with Katia or Hailee would help her feel comfortable enough to sleep. He needed sleep, too. He could always leave with her and go back to his house to sleep.

"Hey, what's Demi doing here?" Simon asked as he walked into the kitchen.

"I have no idea. She surprised me, too," he responded.

"What do you mean, she surprised you? Didn't you stay with her last night?" he asked incredulously.

"No, she said she was fine, so I went home."

"You went home? Left her alone in a house that had just been broken into the day before after she spent all day cleaning it up? Your neighbor was left bleeding on her doorstep. How could you think that was a good idea?" Simon looked at him with derision.

Oliver saw the others working around him, staring at the two of them, listening in to everything they were saying. Screw the dough! He couldn't do this here. "Don't you all have anything better to do? Get back to work. And someone come over here and finish off this dough," he ordered his crew. "My office. Now!" Oliver growled at Simon.

He stalked to his office, Simon following behind. Closing the door with a slam, Oliver started pacing his small office, leaving Simon to stand at the closed door, his arms crossed as he glared at him.

"I know I screwed up, Simon. I knew it last night, but she said she was fine. Why is that something women say all the time and don't mean? I wanted to go over to her house and almost did several times. But I couldn't make myself disturb her. I barely slept thinking about what she was going through in that house, that I came in early. I didn't expect her to come in. I was going to call Katia or Hailee and see if they'd check on her. Maybe stay with her or take her somewhere else to get her mind off what happened. But then she came to work. And that just made me feel worse. She tried to cover it up with makeup, but I can tell she got no more sleep than I did last night with the bags under her eyes. And don't you dare tell her I noticed them. I don't have a death wish. I already screwed up enough as it is," he bit out, pointing a finger at his brother.

At Oliver's impassioned speech, Simon relaxed, his shoulder leaning against the door, his arms uncrossed and his hands in his pockets. "So what are you going to do to fix it?"

"I don't know!" he yelled. "And stop giving me that damn

smirk. Yes, you were right that I was going to mess everything up with her. Now I'm not sure she'll even talk to me anymore for me to fix it."

He deflated at that, sinking into the chair behind his desk. Oliver really wanted to fix what he did to Demi. He loved her so much, but just couldn't seem to get out of his own head to show her.

"Give her some time. I'll see if Aylin and the girls can help talk you up so you can make this right."

"Do you think that will work?"

"No idea, but it can't hurt. Besides, she needs someone right now. And no, that wasn't a dig at you. I'd be the last person to talk about messing things up with the woman you love after everything I did with Aylin."

Oliver remembered how it was when Simon was so confused about how he felt about Aylin. He practically told her she didn't matter to him to her face. Then, he almost lost her for good after a stalker came after her, kidnapping her in Aylin's resort cabin, but not until after the stalker had someone else hit her in the woods, leaving her severely injured. It wasn't pretty, to say the least. But they worked through it with the help of the cousins.

Now they were married.

"I know. Thanks, Simon. Any help would be great. Tell the girls I'll do anything to get her back—even stay away for a while if that's what she needs."

After Simon left, promising to see what he could to help him and Demi, Oliver realized he still had dough fragments all over his hands. It was probably all in his hair by now. Walking out of his office, he went to the small bathroom to wash his hands and make sure he didn't have dough anywhere else.

Maybe staying out of Demi's way until he heard from the girls was a good idea. He didn't want to make things worse than they already were.

33

It had been three days since Demi had spoken with Oliver. Oh, she saw him at work, saying hello in the morning and goodnight when she left in the afternoon. But that was the extent of their conversations. It looked as though he wanted to say something else, but she wasn't ready to talk to him yet.

She threw herself into her work to forget, but the nights were worse. That was when she wished he were with her. But they seemed to have drifted apart, and she couldn't seem to figure out how it happened. She loved him enough to let him go. One thing she didn't want was a relationship with someone who wasn't sure they loved or wanted her.

Today, Demi had a scheduled day off from work and was at her house with Katia and Emma. She didn't know Emma well but was feeling like she was becoming a good friend.

She asked them over to help her go through some more of her parents' stuff in the attic since she was still a little afraid of being by herself. It was the last thing she needed to do in the house. Thankfully, the men who broke in didn't make it up into the attic. Mrs. Tepen made sure of that when she called out to them from outside the front door. Demi was still feeling a little guilty about how she got hurt, but was happy to hear she was doing well at her daughter's house.

"Thanks for coming to help. This is a little overwhelming to do on my own, especially after we cleaned up the entire house when it was wrecked," she said to them as they climbed the stairs to the attic.

"No problem. We're happy to help," Emma said.

"I'm just glad you weren't here when they broke in," Katia added.

Demi's whole body involuntarily shivered. It was a major fear right out of her nightmares. She was still worried they would come back while she was in her home, and that was one reason why she asked them over to help.

"So where do you want us to start?" Katia asked.

Demi looked around the attic space. It was tall enough to stand in the center, with the sides angling down with the roof line. But it covered the entire length of the house like a long, wide hallway.

Her father had put down plywood when they first bought the place to handle whatever her mother wanted to store up here without the risk of falling through to the rooms below. Now, about half of the attic was full of boxes, if they were to stack them on one side of the attic that was. Right now, the boxes were scattered throughout.

"Those boxes at the end were already here when I moved in. We can save those for later. I'm more concerned with getting through the boxes I brought with me from my parents' house in Maryland. I want to make sure there isn't anything in them that belongs to any of their clients. They were just boxed up quickly, especially from my parents' office. And some things I grabbed from the rest of their house may not be worth keeping." She pointed out the rows of stacked boxes to Katia and Emma that were lining the far wall and the stack at the other end of the attic space.

"I'll take this stack. Emma, maybe you want to take those, and Demi, you can take the ones at the end. Ready? Let's go!" Katia said at their nods.

Demi and Emma looked at each other with a little chuckle before moving on to their assigned areas. Katia was usually a little more mild-mannered, but her exuberance was something that sometimes rubbed off from her sister, Ryleigh. Being the middle child of triplets, Katia was the mediator and sometimes took on traits from her more subdued sister, Marinda, and the wild-child, Ryleigh. It was fun to experience. You never knew what you'd get with her.

The three spoke little as they methodically went through one box at a time. Occasionally, Katia or Emma would ask about a particular item, but they mostly kept to themselves to work.

"Hey, Demi, what do you think is on this?" Emma called out, holding up a flash drive in one hand, while holding some sort of journal or notebook in the other.

"I don't know. Maybe we can go look. Which box did you find it in?" Demi said, walking over to her.

"It actually fell out of this journal book. The journal is just a bunch of numbers," Emma said.

Demi took the journal and thumbed through it. "It looks like they might be some of my parents' accounting books. Maybe the flash drive is more of that." She looked at her watch. "We've been up here for a couple of hours. I don't know about you both, but I'm hot and tired. Plus, it's almost lunchtime. Let's take a break and look at this before we eat."

The others agreed, and they slowly made their way down the attic stairs carrying the items they designated to bring down with them: the accounting book and flash drive, some books, a lamp, and some kitchen supplies. Once they got themselves and the items down, Demi grabbed her laptop and carried it into the living room where Katia and Emma were sitting.

Thank goodness her laptop wasn't broken or stolen when her house was burglarized. She was actually surprised it was still in one piece when she started cleaning up. The men who broke in probably covered it up with the clothes they were throwing around and didn't see it.

While she was in her room getting the laptop, Katia went into the kitchen to grab them all some water, placing the bottles on the coffee table for each of them. Emma put together a plate of crackers with cheese and meat for them to munch on to hold them over until lunch.

They settled in the living room on the couch and put the flash drive into her computer. A bunch of files popped up that were confusing to her, along with some folders that were numbered. "Do these look like dates to you?"

"Yeah. See, this one looks like it was from earlier last year. Year and month. Maybe some sort of journal or photos?" Emma said.

Demi clicked on the folder that Emma had pointed out. The files in the folder also looked like dates—maybe the days of the month that the file showed. Clicking the first file in the folder, she realized it was a journal entry. Her eyes widened at what she was reading.

It was written as a personal account from some guy about a bunch of information like things he'd done, such as breaking into places, roughing up people, and killing them.

"What were your parents into?" Katia asked, her eyes as wide as Demi's.

How did they get this and why? Maybe her parents were reporters? Or agents of some kind? It wouldn't be far-fetched. They lived near Washington, D.C., and had lots of clients in high-ranking positions in the city.

"You need to call Luke," Katia said.

Demi knew she was right. Both Katia and Emma were

looking at her with concern. Picking up her phone, she called Luke and asked him to come over as soon as possible.

"He'll be here after he finishes up what he's doing," she told the others after she hung up. "We should probably go back up into the attic and grab the box these were in. What if there's something else in it? I'm not sure I want it in my house."

"Do you think this is why those men broke into your house?" Emma asked.

"I don't know, and I'm not sure I want to know. I'll go up, grab the box and hand it down to you." She walked back over to the attic access and climbed the stairs. From the top, she yelled down, "Which box was it, Emma?"

"The small one sitting open on top of the little table against the far wall," she yelled up.

Seeing the box, Demi walked over to it, peering inside. It looked like there were other journals, some photos, and some old CDs. She hoped none of these items were like the other things they found. She wasn't sure if she could handle more. It was nonstop chaos after her parents died. Grabbing the box, she passed it down to Emma and went back down the stairs. Demi took the box back from Emma, and the three of them went back to the couch to sit down.

"Let's go through this box before Luke gets here. Just in case there's something else we need to give him," Katia suggested.

"That's a good idea. I'm a little scared of what we might find though," Demi said.

"Better to find it and hand it over than have it sitting here in your house," Emma added.

That was true. She wanted nothing to encourage the men to come back to her house. If she gave it to Luke, all the better. "Okay, let's dive in."

34

Luke didn't know what the fuck was going on, but he was fucking tired of whoever was targeting Demi-Lyn Shaw. And he was pissed that he couldn't figure out who was behind all the incidents against her. He had made a call to some of his contacts to help, but they had been out of range for the last week. They were supposed to be back soon, and he hoped they had the information he needed to clear this up.

Luke could admit when he needed help. He was used to working with a team, where they all had each other's backs. Being the sheriff sucked in that respect. He was the top guy, and everyone below him didn't want to rock the boat. Oh, they were good men and women working for him, but it wasn't the same as having a team working together on a problem.

He didn't know what this latest call from Demi-Lyn was about, but if he didn't solve this issue soon, he was going to go fucking ballistic.

Demi-Lyn let Luke into her house when he arrived. She looked nervous. What she found must have really rattled her. His cousin, Katia, was also present, along with a family friend, Emma.

"Hey Demi-Lyn. Katia, Emma. You said you found something important. Care to explain?" he asked once they were all sitting in her living room. The girls were on the couch, while he took the recliner next to them.

"We were looking through my parents' stuff in the attic. The boxes I brought down from their Maryland house. Most of the stuff was photos and other things my parents kept as keepsakes. But some were also from my parents' office," Demi-Lyn began explaining.

"I started going through another box that Demi had previously put aside to go through later," Emma said.

"Why did you put it aside?" he asked Demi-Lyn.

"It looked to be mostly papers and other stuff from my parents' office, so I figured it would take me longer to go through everything. I wasn't sure if there was paperwork that belonged to some of their clients. I was going to contact their lawyer later and send anything I found to return to them."

This had him interested. She brought down papers that potentially belonged to her parents' clients. What did they do again? Oh yeah. They were accountants. Luke thought that might explain someone coming after Demi-Lyn. What if she had something that she shouldn't have? "What was it that made you call me?"

"When I picked up one journal in the box, a flash drive fell out of it," Emma said.

"We figured it might be more photos or something," Katia added.

"My mother liked to do our genealogy and saved old photos and family trees on her computer. We found a bunch of them in other boxes," Demi-Lyn said.

"But this was different." Luke concluded. All three nodded. "Show me."

Emma first handed the journal over to him. He thumbed through it and couldn't make any sense of it. It just looked like a bunch of numbers to him, but Demi-Lyn's parents were accountants, so it made sense. Setting it aside, he asked, "What else?"

Demi-Lyn handed him her laptop and opened it to some files. "Go ahead and click through the files, but this is the first one we opened," she said, pointing to a file on the top of the list.

Luke clicked the file open and read. His demeanor got darker and darker as he read.

What the fuck!

He closed out that file and glanced through some of the other files, then closed out the drive and removed the flash drive. This wasn't good. At all!

He thought he had a better idea of why someone would target Demi-Lyn. But hell if he knew how to stop it. Luke needed to take this in and have someone look at it. Preferably his contacts. They'd decipher what was in the journal and find out if it was attached to these files.

And then they'd start tracking down who the files belonged to and stop them from continuing to harass Demi-Lyn.

"Anything else?" At their negative reply, he told them he needed to go. "I'm going to take these in for evidence. Demi, you need to be careful. Everything that has been happening to you may be connected to this. You need to be careful," he repeated.

Luke knew that shortening her name to Demi instead of calling her Demi-Lyn like he usually did would catch her attention and make her realize how serious this was. From her widened eyes, she got the message. "I'm going to put a deputy outside your house to watch over you. Let the deputy know if you need to go anywhere. He'll follow you and make sure you're safe."

He was scaring Demi-Lyn, but he needed her to be safe. Walking to the kitchen, Luke made a phone call to request a deputy on site. He'd stay until the deputy arrived, then see about getting in touch with his contacts. It was now imperative he reached them—more than ever.

<hr>

Phillip Heaton sat in his penthouse office, staring out at the skyline, as he listened to the men he had sent to take care of the woman and retrieve his property. This whole thing had become a clusterfuck! They couldn't get anything right.

"Tell me again why I don't have my property and the woman is not dead?" he asked deceptively calm.

"Boss, the old woman next door interrupted us when we were searching her house. We almost had it, but she called the cops."

He gripped the phone tightly in his hand, his knuckles whitening as he spoke through clenched teeth. "I don't care if the cops were coming or a whole band was marching through the house. I. Want. My. Property. Prepare the cabin for my arrival. If you can't do the job right on your own, then I'll make sure you can."

He hung up on them, then took a hammer out of a drawer and used it to smash the phone into pieces, shoving the pieces into the same drawer. Throwing the hammer back in and closing the drawer, he pushed the button on his intercom. "I need you in my office. Now."

"Yes, Mr. Heaton," the woman on the other end answered.

The door to his office opened, and a young woman hesitantly entered, a notepad and pen in her hands. She walked to the middle of the room, leaving some room between herself and his desk. She waited patiently for him to begin.

"Cancel all my appointments for the rest of the week."

"Would you like me to reschedule them, sir?"

"No, just cancel them. If I wanted them rescheduled, I

would have said to reschedule them. Why do I keep hiring incompetent people?" he muttered to himself, vowing to make some changes in his business as soon as he returned. "Call to have my plane ready to go tonight."

"Yes, sir." The woman turned and walked out of the office, closing the door once he looked back down at his paperwork, effectively dismissing her.

Opening up the same drawer again, Phillip pulled out another burner phone and dialed. "I'm leaving on a trip tonight. I need you to take care of my receptionist once I'm gone. Make sure it's an accident."

At the affirmative response, he once again took out the hammer, smashing the phone. They would have one last chance and then they were done. He would have them grab the girl and bring her to him. He'd force the information about the item from her himself.

Once he had his property, he'd kill all three of them...dump them into the lake and leave before anyone even knew he was there.

Throwing the phone pieces and hammer back into the drawer, he returned to the paperwork he was trying to complete prior to the call from those imbeciles he sent to Florida.

35

After pulling up to her house, Demi got out of her Jeep, the deputy assigned to her pulling up and parking to the side of the street within watching distance. Waving at him to acknowledge she saw him, the deputy exited his car and walked over to where she was about to reach in for some groceries. It had been a week since she'd had someone following her around everywhere she went. It was annoying, but she also felt safer than she had in a long time.

"Here, let me help you with those," the deputy said.

"I can get it, Pedro," she replied.

"I know you can, but I want to check out your home real quick and make sure it's safe for you to go in. Might as well help while I'm at it," Pedro said.

"Shouldn't you leave your hands free just in case?" she asked.

"I'm good. Maybe just don't give me the bag with eggs in case I need to drop them quickly," he said wryly.

Demi liked Deputy Pedro Galdos. He was young, but professional. He flirted with her, but not in an over-the-top way. It was subtle enough that she figured his carefree attitude was part of his personality. She didn't get the sense that he was an egotistical jerk who thought so highly of himself that he believed his flirting would result in anything. He was just a fun guy who enjoyed talking to people. She witnessed the same jovial flirting with the 60-year-old woman as Demi checked out at the grocery store.

It was a bit of a pain having someone following her everywhere she went, but she admitted it made her feel safer. And having someone as upbeat as Deputy Galdos around didn't hurt.

"Okay, Deputy Prince Charming, here you go," she said teasingly, passing him a bag.

He shook his head at her with a smirk, took her keys after holding out his hand for them, and walked to her front door. Demi followed him in after grabbing the other bag and closing up her Jeep. He'd drop off the bag before checking out the house, so she left him to do his job as they passed by each other in the kitchen.

Putting down her own bag, his cautious steps as he went through each room reached the kitchen, making her feel safer than she wanted to admit. Removing each item from the bags, she put the cold food away, leaving the pantry items on the counter, and was folding up the reusable bags as the deputy returned.

"I'm going to walk around your property real quick, then go back to my car. Lock the door behind me. And remember, my replacement will be here in a couple of hours. I think Nina's scheduled for tonight."

"Thank you, Deputy Galdos."

He nodded to her before walking to the front door, Demi following to lock up behind him. Once that was done, she went back into the kitchen to finish putting away the groceries.

As she organized the items in her pantry, the deputy walked around the perimeter of her property. When he was done, he would go back to his patrol car to sit and watch the house until the other deputy came to relieve him.

Deputy Nina Ashford wouldn't let her know when she arrived, but she would also do a quick walk around her property before going back to her patrol car for her watch.

Even though she wasn't happy that she needed someone watching over her twenty-four seven, she felt a lot safer. She slept better at night. Or as well as possible without Oliver by her side.

Not wanting to think about Oliver yet, Demi shifted her thoughts to her parents. It still hurt so much that they were gone. So many times she wanted to pick up the phone and talk to them. But she couldn't. Now she needed to think about what she had just learned.

Her parents had documentation in their office that would put someone in jail for a long time. Did they really die in an accident? Was everything she thought a lie? Demi just needed to come to terms with the fact that they might have been involved in something that led to their deaths—and put her in danger.

Staring out the window, she looked out over the lake. As a child, she and her father would walk down to their dock and sit on the edge. They would sometimes talk, but most of the time they'd just sit together quietly and think. She wondered if it was still a good place to sit and think, even without her father sitting with her.

Leaving the rest of the groceries next to the empty folded-up bags, she decided she'd be safe enough sitting on her own dock. The deputy was sitting right in front of her house.

He wouldn't be able to see her, though.

That thought made her pause at the sliding glass door. But it wasn't as though she was going away from her property. If something happened, he'd hear her, or she'd run to him. She had her phone with her, too. Grabbing her phone out of her purse, Demi stuck it in the pocket of her jeans before walking out the glass door.

As she walked down the slope of her lawn toward the lake and dock, Demi looked over at Oliver's home and couldn't help but think about him. She was confused about what was going on with him. It seemed one minute he wanted her and the next he didn't.

She was so in love with Oliver Kerrigan. She really didn't know how not to love him. What would she do if he didn't love her? Could she stay in this house when he practically lived next door to her if she never had him fully in her life?

At that moment, she didn't know if she could do it. She would need to move to another house at the very least. Maybe even find another job. She couldn't avoid him totally. Demi was too entrenched with his family. His cousin, Katia, was her best friend. She would be invited to Kerrigan family events and hang out with him at other family gatherings.

She'd see him and feel the intense pain of loving him without actually having him in her life. She may have no choice but to move out of Cypress Bay. That thought depressed her. She didn't want to leave. She wanted Oliver in her life. If she were honest, Demi wanted to live with him, marry him, and create a life together. Children weren't high on her list of wants, but she wouldn't mind if he really wanted them. Maybe.

She just wasn't sure what it was he wanted.

Demi approached the lake and looked around. The resort on the far end of the lake, with its cabins dotted amongst the trees, was barely visible on the shoreline. People were on the lake in the boats giving tours and rented out by Joel Madris, his shop next door to the resort and their cabins. Most would be returning the boats as the sun was setting. Katia told her that Joel didn't like having his equipment out at night other than for the night tours some of his employees gave.

Thankfully, the people vacationing in Cypress Bay stayed

closer to the resort and town side of the lake and stayed away from the side of the lake with private neighborhoods and houses.

Demi walked down to her dock, crossing her legs in front of her, as she sat on the side looking away from the resort and people. She wanted peace to think, and the calmness of her side of the lake was just what she needed.

It was darker out here, except for the soft glowing lights of the bridge further down the lake that connected one end of the county to the other.

Some dock lights were also shining around the lake—her own included—but many were low-level lighting, giving a slight glow, but not bright enough to interfere with the peace and quiet of the lake. The sounds of the resort and boat shop were a distant drone, but even that was quieting down as the sun set.

Pulling out her mother's rosary beads, Demi fiddled with them in her hand as she leaned back to watch as the sun set and some stars were barely visible in the sky. As the sun got lower, the moon became more prominent, giving a relaxing glow over the lake.

Her whole body relaxed right along with it. This was where she needed to be; she just hoped she could stay.

Deep in thought, Demi stared down at the rosary beads in her hand and wished her mother was still with her. And that her father was sitting next to her to give Demi the strength she needed to get through everything going wrong in her life.

No, not wrong, she thought.

Her life was pretty good if she took away the death of her parents, someone shooting at her and breaking into her house, and Oliver stepping away from her.

Okay, never mind. Not so good after all. But she had her friends, a nice house on the lake, the old Jeep was still running, and she had a job she enjoyed. So maybe it balanced out. She'd need to think about whether the good outweighed the bad.

Hearing a noise behind her, she paused, running her fingers through her mother's rosary beads, and listened. What was that thump?

She turned around to see what made the noise when a hand came across her body and another came up to her face, holding something over her nose and mouth. Demi struggled, dropping the rosary beads onto the dock as someone lifted her onto her feet.

"Gotcha now, bitch," she heard from the man behind her right before everything went dark.

36

"What are you still doing here?" Oliver looked up from the menu he was creating to see his father standing at the door to his office.

He was asking himself the same question. What was he still doing at work? He used the excuse of needing to work on the new menu, but it wasn't as though he was actually working on it right now. He was just sitting at his desk thinking about Demi.

"Hey, Dad. What are you doing here?" he asked his father. He was so glad to see his father begin to live his life again. The last year had been hell for all of them, but even more so for his father. Losing Oliver and Simon's mother was a blow to them all. His father totally lost it, though. Lauren Kerrigan was John's soulmate and the love of his life. They were slated to travel together after John had signed over his portion of the resort to him and Simon.

Then, she was killed by a drunk driver on her way home from dropping her parents off at the airport in Orlando. His father had obviously not taken it well. He caused a lot of chaos

200

at the resort, putting him and Simon through the ringer trying to help him get his act together.

But now, a year later, his father was doing much better. He was helping at the resort without impeding the other employees. Oliver was especially happy to see his father be able to talk about his mother more without falling down into a deep pit of despair.

"I was just leaving. Saw your light on and wondered why you weren't over at Demi's spending some time with her," his father said.

Damn...did he need to bring up Demi? Oliver was being a dumbass. He didn't need his father to point it out to him, even if it was in an offhanded way.

"Look, I know I screwed up, okay? I'm just going to finish this up, then I'm going home. Tomorrow, I'll see about talking to Demi," he said to his father. He needed some time to work out a plan so that she would talk to him again. He didn't want to only tell her that he loved her. She needed one hell of an apology, too.

"Don't wait too long or make excuses, Oliver. You know that nothing in life is guaranteed, so why waste a single moment of the time that you have left with her? I only wish I hadn't invested so much time in this resort at the beginning of my years with your mother. I missed some important time with her I'll never get back now. Don't make the same mistake." And with that, his father walked out of his office, leaving Oliver to stare after him.

It was so clear to him he needed Demi. Full stop. No other thought than that was in his head.

He needed her in his life, in his house, in his bed. And he'd done nothing but give her conflicting messages. He needed to fix this with her because he couldn't live the rest of his life without her. He'd been going crazy seeing her at work, but not actually being able to talk to her, spend time with her. Oliver thought it would be enough only to see her at work, that he needed nothing else from her. But he just couldn't live his life without Demi.

He was not an emotionally stunted man! He just felt too much and needed to keep it locked down or he'd explode. Yet Demi made him feel more, and in a good way. She calmed him when he felt too much, especially when he felt like he'd break whenever he thought about losing his mother. Demi lost everyone and everything in her life, yet could move forward and start again. He lost his mother, but he still had the rest of his family, a job that he loved, everything—except Demi.

Now he needed her!

Standing up from his desk, Oliver grabbed his keys and ran out of his office, down the short hallway to the back door. First, he'd stop by his house to change and shower, then go to her house. He wouldn't let her turn him away. He needed to make this right. The last thing he wanted to do was survive another night without her by his side. He'd been sleeping like crap, and he knew she was, too. That ended tonight!

As he drove past her house, Oliver waved to the deputy sitting in his car watching Demi's house. He didn't like that she had to have protection around her all the time. Luke had told him about what she had found. Well, he didn't really tell him a whole lot of anything, to be honest. He said Demi, Katia, and Emma had found something incriminating in her parents' boxes, and now she had to have protection until Luke found out what was going on. Oliver should have gone to her then, but he didn't. He'd rectify that now.

Parking his car in his driveway, Oliver got out and walked over to the deputy. Screw the shower first. He had to see Demi. "Pedro. How's it going?"

"Hey, Oliver. Everything's good. Your girl is all in for the night. Went grocery shopping, then came home. I did a walk-through of her home and property before coming back to the car," Pedro answered.

His girl. Yes, that was what he wanted. Everyone else accepted it as a fact, so now it was his turn to convince Demi.

"Good to hear. I'm heading over to see for myself." Oliver turned and walked to her home.

"About time," Pedro muttered.

Oliver heard what he said, but wasn't about to take the time to find out what he meant by that. Of course, he knew. Everyone had been giving him a hard time for not making things right with Demi.

At the door, he knocked and waited to hear her walking to let him in. Not hearing anything, he knocked again, this time louder. He waited a few more minutes and, when he still heard nothing, looked around. Her lights were on, but the curtains were drawn, so he couldn't see inside. Maybe she knew it was him and was ignoring him. Or she was being cautious.

Of course, she wasn't answering the door. She had someone after her and had security around her all day. Oliver mentally kicked himself before pulling out his phone, bringing up her name in his contacts. The phone rang several times. Pulling it away from his ear, he listened through the door for some sort of response, but again heard nothing. He quickly typed out a text letting her know it was him at the door. But there was still no response. He wasn't surprised. She frequently forgot to turn her ringer back on after work.

Taking a quick look at the deputy, he shrugged his shoulders to show he wasn't sure why Demi wasn't answering her door and phone. Maybe she fell asleep? She hadn't been sleeping much lately, but Pedro said he had just left her not too long ago. Was it enough time for her to fall asleep?

The deputy sat up straighter in his seat with his shrug, but he couldn't wait to see what he would do. Making his way around the house, the drapes weren't drawn on the sliding glass door, allowing him to peek inside. Empty grocery bags and a few pantry items were sitting on the counter waiting to be put away. But still no Demi in sight.

As he was wrestling with whether to open the glass door to check on her, Pedro stepped around the corner of her house.

"What's going on?" he asked Oliver.

"I'm not sure. She wasn't answering her door or phone. No surprise since she has you hanging around for a reason. But I don't see her anywhere. She didn't put all her groceries away, and the lights are still on. Demi may have fallen asleep, though. I was just trying to decide whether I wanted to break into her house to check on her or not."

The deputy walked up to the back of the house and peered into the kitchen. He reached for the glass door, both of them surprised it was unlocked and opened easily.

"Stay out here. I'm going to check it out," Deputy Galdos said as he unhooked the loop on his gun, placing his hand on the butt. He walked carefully into the house.

Oliver watched as Pedro searched the kitchen and living room area, then disappeared down the hallway. Minutes later, he came back, stepping outside and closing the glass door.

"She's not inside," he said.

"Maybe she went down to the dock? I know she enjoys sitting down there to think."

"Demi wasn't supposed to leave the house without telling me first. She has my number and should have texted," the deputy said disgruntled.

"She must have forgotten. Come on, let's go walk down to the dock. She's probably staring up at the stars. Then you can yell at her. I'll tell you to knock it off and be the hero," he said with amusement.

The deputy chuckled. "Deal."

They walked to the dock together, prepared to see Demi sitting or lying on it. Instead, it was empty.

"She's not here. Would she walk along the lake?" Pedro asked.

"No, she likes to sit on the dock," he replied. Oliver was getting a bad feeling. This couldn't be happening. Walking down to the end of the dock, he saw her mother's rosary beads sitting in the middle of the boards. She always had them on her. Demi would never leave it lying around on the dock.

Oliver felt uneasy and started frantically calling out for her. "Demi! Demi, where are you? Yell out if you're hurt. I can come to you."

There was no answer.

"I'll call this in." Pedro unhooked his radio and contacted dispatch to report Demi missing.

Oliver stood at the end of the dock, staring at the rosary beads barely illuminated by the dock lights.

Please be all right. He didn't know what he'd do without her.

37

Slowly waking up, Demi felt groggy, and her head hurt. It throbbed as if she had drunk too much the night before and had a massive hangover. The problem was she hadn't been drinking. Did she have an accident and hit her head? Her head was muddled with fragmented thoughts pinging around, trying to figure out what was going on. And her whole body felt heavy, too, making it hard to move or open her eyes.

Giving up on trying to open her eyes—she was so tired—Demi kept her eyes closed while using her other senses. It didn't smell like her home. There was a more masculine scent in the air. A combination of aftershave and sweat. Was she at Oliver's house? No, his house didn't smell like this. His home usually smelled like a citrusy musk mixed with whatever recipe he was currently trying out. This was a sour smell. It didn't smell like a hospital.

Where was she?

It took Demi a moment to realize something else. She wasn't lying down. Instead, she was sitting up on a hard surface with something wrapped tight around her. Her head drooped and was too heavy for her to lift.

Panic started building inside that whatever was happening to her wasn't right.

"Where is my property?" a man growled, startling her. Demi didn't even consider that she wasn't alone.

She forced herself to open her eyes, though they wanted to remain closed. The last thing she wanted right now was for reality to intrude. This was probably just a bad dream, and any minute she'd wake up. When Demi finally opened her eyes, she knew this wasn't a dream.

Demi's blurry eyes tried to focus on the man in front of her. He had on an immaculately tailored gray suit, his feet planted firmly, his arms crossed. Looking further up, she thought others would think him handsome with a chiseled jawline, slightly tanned skin, chocolate brown eyes, and neatly styled dark hair. But it was the look in his eyes that scared the shit out of her. This was not a man someone crossed.

"Where. Is. My. Property," he repeated.

"What?" she slurred. "I d-don't know what you're talking about. Where am I?"

Before she could track his movements, the man uncrossed his arms and slapped her hard across the face. The slap echoed through the room as her head jerked to the right from the force.

Owww! What the hell! That hurt. Demi didn't know what was going on. What did this man think she had and why was he asking her? Her head wasn't the only thing that throbbed now. Her cheek felt like it was on fire. She didn't like being hit, but it did one thing for her. She was no longer feeling out of it. The man asked about his property. Damn. Was this the person who wanted the items she gave to Luke? If so, she was in real trouble.

Trying to stay awake, she figured out a couple of things. First, she was tied to a chair with some sort of rope wrapping her arms to her waist and the back of the chair, and at her ankles to the corners of the chair legs.

Second, she was in a cabin. Wispy curtains on the windows and rustic furniture made it seem like someone was trying too hard to make it feel like they were in the country instead of a lakeside cabin. The sun was rising, its muddled light coming through the windows, and she could vaguely hear the sounds of people just getting out onto the water. It should have made her happy that she most likely wasn't very far from the lake, but there were a ton of cabins and homes, many of them rentals.

She had to have a plan to escape. If only she'd be able to think straight enough. Maybe she should just play dumb about the property the man was talking about to buy herself more time. Hopefully, Luke was aware she was missing by now and was looking for her.

"Now let's try this again. You have something that belongs to me, and I want it back."

Turning her head slowly toward the man, she noticed there were two other men standing on the other side of the room near the door, as if on guard. She was in serious trouble.

"I don't know what you want. I don't have your property."

"You don't know what I'm talking about? Well, let me jog your memory then. Your parents stole some important things from me. When I demanded they give them back, they ignored me and tried to leave instead. So, I had them killed. My men searched their home in Maryland, but someone had already cleaned it out. Do you know who that person was?" he asked deceptively calm.

When she didn't answer, he continued. "No? Well, I want what they took back. And I think you're the one who took my property. You'll tell me where you put it, and once I have it, I'm going to kill you."

Demi was really shaking now. This man wasn't fooling around, and the thought of dying had her scared enough to want to hide.

"I'm going to give you some time to think about the

consequences of not telling me where my property is located. When I come back, you'll tell me everything, or I'll make you tell me. Understand?" At her hesitant nod, the man exited the room, the other men following him, slamming the door closed behind them.

She was shocked to realize what she had been suspecting was true...her parents' death was not an accident. This was a serious situation, and she needed to escape soon. Demi couldn't wait for Luke to find her.

What if no one knew she was missing yet? The deputy watching her house left her safe inside. She was an idiot for going out the back to the dock where he couldn't see her. Had the new deputy who took over noticed her lights were never turned off? Would she have investigated to find out why? Or did she stay in her patrol car after being told Demi was all right inside for the night?

No one would come to the door until Deputy Galdos came back in the morning. The sun was just coming up now. It could be another hour before he realized she was gone. How long would it take for Luke to get the message and start looking for her? It was the only question she had an answer for—too long.

It was up to her to save herself. But how?

Looking around, she couldn't see anything helpful. The room was bare other than a bed in the corner that had a headboard made of branches, and a dresser. Besides, she was bound to a chair in the middle of the room. She reached up with her hands to move the rope around her upper arms and waist, but it wouldn't budge. Dropping her hands, she felt something hard in her pocket.

You are an idiot, Demi; she said to herself once she realized the men who kidnapped her didn't tie up her hands nor did they check her pockets. The rope was too tight, and she couldn't reach the knot that was behind her. So untying her ankles would be out, but apparently they didn't realize she had her cell phone in her pocket. If she could just reach in and pull it out.

Demi struggled to twist herself enough to reach into her pocket for the phone. The pockets on her jeans were not angled, so it took a little effort to reach them. While her hands were not tied, the rope held her arms back. She felt the rope dig into her upper arms as she tried to rotate them more toward the front so she could reach her pocket.

Wait...could she try to get her arms out from beneath the ropes? If even one of them was out, she might be able to reach her ankles to untie them, and it would also loosen up the rope around her waist.

Bending her elbow so her right hand was bent up, Demi tried to wiggle her hand up and under the rope around her waist and upper arms. It was an extremely tight fit. She hoped her hand wouldn't get stuck under the rope. That's all she would need...to have her hand also stuck so she couldn't reach her phone.

Using her left hand to pull the rope away from her as much as possible and sucking her breath in, she squeezed her hand under the rope. Tucking her elbow in, she straightened her elbow to remove her arm from the rope. The rope scraped and tore at her skin as it went through, but her arm was free.

Not wanting to push her luck, Demi finally pulled out her phone and turned it on—muffling it against her to prevent anyone from hearing the carrier's jingle. When it was finally connected, she saw a few calls and texts from Oliver. She skimmed the texts, ignoring the calls for now. No need to push her luck.

> Oliver: Hey, Demi. It's me at the door. I understand why you're ignoring my knocks. But can I talk to you? Please.

> Oliver: Are you sleeping and forgot to turn out your lights?

Some time passed before the next texts.

She was thankful someone realized she was missing and her phone was off. If the men had heard her phone ring or vibrate, she might not have it now to send a message for help. But what could she tell them so they'd be able to find her? She didn't know where she was.

Demi typed out what she knew as quickly as possible. She didn't know how long she had before the men came back, and she didn't want them to take her phone. If they found out someone was looking for her and she texted them, she was as good as dead. Well, she was going to die no matter what if she wasn't found anyway, but they would kill her sooner if they knew someone was looking for her. These men were not playing around.

After hitting send, Demi waited a moment to see if there was a response, then put the phone back into her pocket and sat back to wait for them to find her.

"Please come for me soon. I'm so scared," she whispered.

38

Early that morning, Oliver was sitting in Demi's living room with Luke, a couple of his deputies, Katia, Simon, and Aylin talking about how to find Demi. They'd been searching all night, and they still couldn't find her. It was as if she had just disappeared. If it hadn't been for finding the rosary beads on the dock, Oliver wasn't sure they'd ever have known she was in danger.

"I received some info from my friends about the items Demi-Lyn gave me," Luke said, looking down at his phone. "They belong to a Phillip Heaton. Apparently, he's a businessman who owns a big company up in Washington, DC. On the outside he's clean. Single, lives in a large home in an area just outside of the city, has a decent-sized bank account, and no prior convictions.

"But the journals and info on the flash drive Demi-Lyn gave me say otherwise. I found out that Demi's parents were contracted with what they thought was his company, but one of Phillip Heaton's lackeys hired them to cook the books. And before anyone asks, they didn't know what they were hired to do. It seems he hired them instead of using his own accounting department to change records after the fact so he could blame them later. Something about paying them back for a political friend who didn't like them telling him no.

"We think they figured it out and started keeping track of everything. They may have been about to turn him in before they died. I wouldn't be surprised if he had them killed. Now Phillip Heaton is most likely trying to get the evidence back before anyone else finds it," Luke said.

"He sent people after her to get the journals and flash drive. And now they have her, but it will not help them get what they want. You have the items they're looking for," Oliver said. This wasn't good. If Phillip Heaton found out Demi turned the items over to Luke, the man might tell those who worked for him to seriously hurt or kill her. The thought scared him.

"Yes, I think they were sent to retrieve the information her parents had about him. They must have known Demi-Lyn brought them with her when she packed up her parent's home in Maryland. I don't think they're going to take a chance of bringing her all the way back to Phillip Heaton. They'd want the items back now, so they'd stay close in case they needed to come back to the house to retrieve them. They probably have her stashed somewhere nearby.

"Her phone isn't pinging. She may have it off, or they destroyed it. But my friends are good at what they do and will find her," Luke promised.

Oliver didn't know who these friends of Luke were, but he hoped they'd find her soon. In the movies, people could be traced by their phones, but Luke saying it was off had him wondering what had happened to it. It may have been dropped somewhere in the woods around the dock before she went missing, or the men may have thrown it into the lake.

That had him thinking about whether she was even taken or if she was lying somewhere injured or dead. They may have killed her because they didn't find what they came for. Or maybe she fell into the water and drowned. Oliver didn't want to even think about what she'd gone through. May still be going through. He was heartbroken about it.

Luke was now on the phone with these mysterious friends of his asking them to look for something. Oliver really didn't have a clue what, and to be honest he didn't care. He just wanted to know where Demi was and that she was all right.

Oliver felt his phone buzz and pulled it out of his pocket. Reading the message, Oliver couldn't believe what he was seeing. It was a message from Demi!

Demi: kidnapped cabin lake 3 men help.

"Luke!" he yelled across the room, holding out his hand with the cell phone as if his cousin could read it from across the room.

Luke, with his phone still held to his ear, strode over and grabbed the phone, reading the text. "She has her phone. Can you trace it?" he asked the person on the other end.

He walked away, Oliver's phone still in his hand, talking rapidly into the phone before hanging up and walking over to his deputies still in the house. "I need you to canvas the area around the lake for the car we had an earlier description of from Mrs. Tepen. Look down every driveway that leads to a cabin on the lake."

Luke walked back over to Oliver, handing him his phone back. "It will only be a moment. They'll pinpoint exactly where Demi-Lyn is now that she has her phone on."

"How do you know that?" he asked. He seemed to count on these people to pull off a miracle in finding her. There were so many cabins around Lake Tola—mostly rented out to tourists and a few occupied by locals.

"Don't worry, my friends are good," Luke said confidently.

Oliver wondered about the kind of friends he had who

could find someone so quickly just by looking for a phone. Luke had been in the military, so maybe he knew them from when he was in the Army? But what type of people had the kind of connections they seemed to have, pinpointing someone's cell phone with no need to ask for permission first? Then again, what did it matter to him as long as they found Demi?

Five minutes later—though it felt like forever to Oliver—Luke got a call back saying they found the location the message was sent from. Luke thanked the person, hung up, then called in to his dispatcher to let his deputies know where to meet him.

Oliver stood, walking toward Luke, Katia coming with him.

"You're not coming. I need you both to stay here," he told them.

Katia relented and sat back down. But there was no way Oliver was going to sit around and wait for him to find Demi.

"I'll stay out of the way, but I'm coming with you." Oliver said, staring down at Luke.

After a moment, Luke backed down. "You need to stay in the car. No getting in the way, understand?" Luke admonished. At his nod, Luke turned and left the house, Oliver following behind.

Please let them find her, Oliver thought before they drove away from her home.

39

Demi wasn't sure whether or not her message was understood. It showed as read almost immediately, but she never got a reply. Still, knowing Oliver knew she was missing and had contacted Luke went a long way to make her feel better. Maybe he couldn't answer because they were on their way to rescue her.

She didn't know how long it had been since she messaged Oliver or when the men had left, though she used the time as wisely as possible. It took some maneuvering that wasn't very comfortable, but Demi untied the ropes around her ankles. It turned out they didn't tie those as tightly as the one around her waist.

Once untied, she wrapped them loosely around her ankles to make it look like she was still tied up. She got her other arm out of the rope around her waist, too. Having her arms out, loosened the rope around her so she could breathe better. And she felt more in control and able to fight back if she had the opportunity.

The sound of the door unlocking had Demi quickly putting her arms and hands back into the position they were in when the rope was around them. She hoped they didn't notice her arms were not under the rope or that they were all scraped up from rope burn.

She watched the man, who was clearly in charge, come in with the other two men following behind him. They again stood at the door as though blocking it. The man walked right up to her, towering over her.

If the other guys were not with him, she'd kick him when he was least expecting it. He was close enough she might even knee him in the balls. That would make her feel better in this whole situation, but she didn't think it would be a good idea to try it. The men with him would most definitely react, and she wouldn't like the outcome.

"Your time is up. Tell me where my property is or I'll make you tell me," he said.

The two men behind him had their hands raised in fists, like they were ready to hurt her. She'd never been so frightened in her life. Even knowing she got a message out to Oliver, and Luke was probably doing everything possible to find her, Demi wasn't sure how long it would take them or if her message made it easier or harder for them.

"I'll tell you where it is. Just don't hurt me! It's in my house, in the boxes I brought down with me from my parents' house," she said, panicking that no one would arrive quickly enough for her. She needed to stall and give Luke more time to find her. Maybe if he thought she was being cooperative, then he'd leave her alone.

The man nodded, and one man walked up and punched her in the face. Owww...that hurt worse than the slap. She would not survive this if they kept this up. Her face and eye were already swelling from the hit.

"Nice try, but that won't work. Your house was already searched, and what belongs to me wasn't found," the man growled at her.

"They didn't look in my attic. I stored some boxes up there

until I could go through them," she slurred. It was getting harder to pay attention to what the man was saying. She could barely see out of her left eye anymore, and the left side of her mouth wouldn't open well.

The man looked at his men. "Did you search the attic?"

One man looked nervous, but stepped up to speak. "The old lady disturbed us, and we had to leave right as we were about to search it."

"Go back to her house, grab everything out of her attic and bring it to me."

"She had a cop watching her. What if they realize she's gone and there are more at the house?" the other man asked, looking nervous.

"I don't care if the place is crawling with cops. I. Want. My. Property. You were supposed to get it for me, and you failed." The man pulled a gun out from under his suit jacket and pointed it at the man in front of him. "If I don't see my property in the next hour, you won't see another day. Got me?"

"Yes, boss," both of the men replied before hightailing it out of the room.

Demi was terrified. Now that she had told him where the items were, would he kill her? What if she told him that was where it used to be, but she found it and gave it to a friend to look at? She couldn't tell him that Luke was the sheriff. He would kill her just as quickly.

Who was she kidding? She was as good as dead. Her attempt to stall the man to give Luke and his deputies more time to find her failed. Even getting herself out of the ropes wouldn't help her. She couldn't outrun the gun he had in his hand.

She would never see Oliver again. It was funny to her that the thought of not seeing him ever again scared her more than dying. She didn't believe in a heaven or hell, though if she did, these men would be in hell at their end. But her mother believed, and Demi wished heaven were true. She'd see her parents again. Let them know she was all right, well as all right as she could be with a homicidal man about to kill her.

Yet all she thought about was Oliver. She loved him so much, and it hurt that he pulled away from her. And now she wouldn't have the chance to tell him how she felt about him, or give him the chance to make it up to her. Maybe with one of his wonderful breakfasts in bed.

He would blame himself when she was gone. Demi couldn't let that happen. She had to survive. She didn't spend all that time loosening her ropes and freeing her arms just to sit still while the man killed her, did she? No! She was going to escape, even if it was the last thing she did.

As the men left and the door closed, the man turned to face her, pointing the gun directly at her. She said she was going to fight, but how could she escape a bullet? Demi worked out a plan in her head. She'd dive to the right as he was getting ready to fire, then kick out at him. Hopefully, that would throw him off just enough for him to lose the gun. It was the only way she had a fighting chance.

The man looked at her and said, "Hmmm. Now the question is whether to make this fast or make you suffer for everything you put me through. I..."

Just as Demi thought it was all be over for her, the door burst open and Luke and his deputies stormed in. The guy shifted closer to her and ran behind her. Knowing she had to do whatever she could to help, she stuck her foot out. The man lurched toward the floor; the gun skittered away toward the other side of the room.

The deputies ran over to the man, securing him quickly before dragging him out of the room.

Luke approached her. "Demi-Lyn, are you all right?"

His eyebrows narrowed as he looked her over. She must look terrible where they hit her, but she was thankful they found her and it wasn't worse. "Yes, I'm fine. I just want to get out of here."

Luke untied the rope from around her waist and looked up in surprise that the others around her ankles weren't tied. "You are strong as fuck, Demi-Lyn. You were probably about to save yourself, weren't you?"

He always summed things up in his own gruff way. Demi always thought it was because of his time spent in the military. And while she preferred her nickname, she was thrilled to be hearing her full name come out of Luke's mouth. It meant that she was safe.

"I was until he pulled the gun out. I was losing hope again right before you came bursting in here. Thank you."

"You never need to thank me. Come on, there's someone outside waiting for you, and then you're going to the hospital to be checked out."

"I don't want to go to the hospital. Can't I just go home?" she asked, totally skipping what he said about someone waiting for her.

"No deal. You're going to the hospital, and that's final."

"Oh! There were two other men. They were going back to my house."

"Don't worry. We got them first, right outside as they were trying to leave. You don't need to be afraid anymore, Demi-Lyn."

Her eyes filled with tears of gratitude for all he had done to help her. And not just him. The entire Kerrigan family had been supporting her since she showed up after her parents died. She would miss him and the other Kerrigans if she had to leave Cypress Bay, she thought as he helped her out of the house. But she would miss Oliver more than anyone.

"Demi!"

Her head snapped up from watching the ground as Luke helped her walk out of the house where she was being held captive. Oliver! He was who was waiting for her? Her hopes rose at seeing him. Maybe there was still hope of making it work. Demi couldn't hold back anymore. She'd tell him she loved him as soon as possible.

Earlier, Oliver sat in the seat next to Luke as he drove quickly through the neighborhoods around the lake before arriving at the location where his contacts told him Demi was being held. He still didn't know how they found her so fast from one text, but he was happy they did.

The entire time he was sending up a silent plea and hoping they would arrive in time. After everything Luke had told them about who was after Demi, he worried they would be too late. What would he do if he lost her? He didn't think he would make it...losing another person so close to his heart. Oliver told himself that when, not if, they found Demi alive, he would do anything and everything to let her know how much he loved her.

The cars had careened down the road and stopped with a jerk at the end of the driveway, just as another car was about to pull out. Oliver had recognized the car as the one Mrs. Tepen had described to them. These were the men who kidnapped Demi.

Luke jumped out of the car after telling him to stay inside, his gun drawn and pointed at the men in the car. His deputies surrounded them, some coming up from behind, where they opened the doors and pulled the men out.

The end was a bit anticlimactic, if he was being honest. No shots fired. Just a lot of yelling from Luke and his deputies to put their hands up and not to move. Then, they were pulled out of the car and handcuffed before being taken away by a couple of deputies. Luke walked back to the car, opened the door and sat down.

"They won't talk, but it isn't hard to figure out that they have her stashed inside the cabin here. We're going to leave our cars here and walk the rest of the way. If there's someone else with Demi-Lyn, we don't want to tip them off by driving in," Luke said.

"Okay. Let's go." Oliver had been ready to see Demi and make sure she was all right.

"You're going to stay here. I mean it, Oliver. I'll bring her to you."

Oliver narrowed his eyes at Luke but didn't argue with him. He'd stay in the patrol car. For now. He wasn't about to make any promises for how long, and Luke knew that. It had to be enough. He didn't want to cause any problems for his cousin or his deputies, and he definitely didn't want to make things worse for Demi. But he also wasn't about to hold out for long before he had to go see her and make sure she was okay.

He had watched Luke and his deputies walk toward the cabin that was hidden down a longer driveway and surrounded by woods before it opened up at the lake. They had all looked at Google Maps to make sure they had the exact layout of the property before leaving Demi's house.

Remembering the rush to drive to their current location, Oliver was still sitting in the patrol car as they disappeared around the corner and were no longer seen. He switched his focus from staring down the driveway to the clock and back again. How much time did they need, anyway?

Five minutes later, he couldn't make himself wait in the car any longer. It was killing him not knowing what was going on or how Demi was doing.

He got out of the car and slowly made his way down the driveway, sticking close to the edge of the woods to make sure he was out of the way and to use the trees as cover if he needed it. He watched police shows sometimes...the people who just stood in the middle of the road were the ones who were run over, shot, or stabbed. If the man holding Demi came racing around the corner trying to escape capture, he didn't want to be out in the open.

He walked cautiously around the corner, where the driveway curved toward the home. The door was wide open; two deputies were flanking the corners, monitoring the front door and sides of the house. He wouldn't be surprised if there were others at the back to make sure no one ran out that way. Oliver didn't see Luke, so he figured he was inside. His cousin would take care of Demi himself.

Oliver knew Luke was as worried about her as he and the rest of the family were. Demi was like another member of the family and always had been—even if they only saw her over the summers growing up.

He also thought Luke was feeling a little guilty that he hadn't realized the previous incidents were more serious than he had made them out to be. Oliver could have told him that no one thought Demi would be kidnapped based on what had happened before. Sure, her property was obviously being targeted, but there was never anything done that targeted her personal safety. Other than Mrs. Tepen being hurt when she interrupted the men breaking into Demi's house, no one else had been hurt in all this.

Trying to keep himself behind some trees so as not to be seen, Oliver watched as one deputy walked out of the house with a furious man in cuffs. The man was glaring at everyone, spouting off something about how they didn't know who he was and that he was going to make sure they all paid for treating him this way.

Then Demi was in the doorway, being helped from the house by Luke, and all of Oliver's focus was on her. She looked like she was okay, but wait—was that a bruise forming on her face? He took a step toward her, calling out her name, "Demi!"

Her head jolted up at hearing him call her name. Damn it! That was a big fucking bruise on her face, and her eye looked to be swelled up, too. If the men who did this weren't already in custody, he would kill them for doing this to her. Before he knew it, he was walking toward her. He had to see what else was wrong, and then take care of her.

Just when he thought all was well, the man in custody broke free from the deputy and ran quickly toward Demi, who didn't see him coming.

"Demi, watch out!" Oliver shouted, but it wasn't soon enough, and Demi was tumbling out of Luke's grasp, falling under the man.

"You'll never be safe from me. It's only a matter of time before you're dead," the man growled at her, his hands still handcuffed behind him. He was lying on Demi as he kicked and kneed her.

Luke rushed to remove him from Demi with the help of the deputy, while Oliver ran over to help her up and make sure she was all right.

41

Shock permeated Demi's entire body. The man she was just rescued from attacked her again. She was currently lying on the ground, unable to get up after the fall. Her whole body felt sore, and her face was throbbing after hitting the ground in the same place where he had hit her before.

The man was cursing obscenities and threatening to kill everyone when they least expected it. He was still fighting Luke and the deputy as they were ushering him into the patrol car.

Closing her eyes, she felt an immense need to sleep for the next twenty-four hours. But she couldn't do it here.

"Are you okay, Demi?" Opening her eyes, Oliver was kneeling by her side, his hands hovering over her as though not sure where it was safe to touch her.

Everything was swirling in her mind. Was this her life now? Would she always need to look over her shoulder, waiting for this guy to kill her? Sure, he was going to jail, but that didn't mean he wouldn't get out and come after her later.

She just wanted to live a simple life and maybe have a future with Oliver...if he wanted her. He'd been so distant lately, but he wasn't acting distant now. Was it possible to really have the type of life she always wanted with him?

"I'll be okay. What are you doing here?" she asked him cautiously. She was confused why he would come to her rescue. He was a chef, not one of Luke's deputies. He shouldn't be anywhere in the area. And she was a little pissed that Luke had let him come along. Oliver could have been hurt.

Besides, she was hoping to have time to clean up and rest before seeing him again. She loved him, but that didn't mean she wanted him to see her like this. Especially considering how hot and cold he'd been lately. Demi just didn't have the bandwidth to have her emotions ping-pong back and forth depending on whether or not he wanted her in any given moment.

"Where else would I be? When the woman I love is kidnapped and sends me a cryptic text message saying she's been taken, I need to make sure she's all right for myself. Do you think you can get up?" he asked quickly, changing the topic. Her head was spinning, and not just because it was pounding.

What did Oliver say? Demi asked herself as she let him help her up. Holding onto his biceps, she tried to stay upright. Her head was spinning now more than ever, but this time it wasn't just because of the hits she took.

Looking up at him, she asked, "You love me?"

He returned a look she thought of as tender and full of love. He really did love her. It was pouring out of him for her and anyone else who looked to see.

"Of course, I love you. How could I not? I'm sorry for how I've been acting lately. I think I've loved you since you first kissed me that last summer twelve years ago," he said, startling her.

"What?" she whispered. Demi didn't know what to think. That was an innocent kiss on a guy she was crushing on when she was fourteen and he was seventeen. She may have loved him since then, but she couldn't see how he'd have felt the same way.

Interrupting her thoughts, Luke came back over to where they were standing. "Are you okay, Demi-Lyn? He shouldn't have been able to get to you."

"I'm good, Luke," she replied.

"She needs to go to the hospital to be checked out," Oliver broke in.

Well, damn it. She thought if she didn't mention it, Luke would forget what he said about going to the hospital. Then Oliver needed to bring it up again. Perfect.

"Oh, no...I'll be good. I want to go home and rest. If you could drop me off, I'll probably just crawl into bed and sleep for a couple of days," she said. Demi looked over and saw the worry on Oliver's face and in his eyes. She reassured him that she was okay. "I'm all right, Oliver, really." She was happy to see he seemed to relax a bit.

"Whether you want to or not, there's an ambulance waiting for you at the end of the driveway. You're going to hop up on the gurney they're bringing and go to the hospital to be checked out, even if I need to tie you to it," Luke said.

She looked at him with her mouth dropped open. Did he just say he was going to tie her to the gurney if she refused to go to the hospital? At Oliver's chuckle next to her, she looked over at him. If he thought this was funny, she would set him straight.

"Please, Demi. If you don't want to do it for you, would you do it for me?" Oliver looked at her as if he was really worried for her. She must look pretty rough after her ordeal. She could admit that her vision was hindered from the swelling in her left eye and her face, and her head continued to throb painfully, and she was feeling dizzy and weak.

"Okay, I'll go. Will you come with me?" she asked.

"You couldn't keep me away," he said.

His words settled deeply inside, calming her down more

than anything else. At least until she thought again about what would happen when the man who kidnapped her was released from jail.

"Umm...Luke. What about the man who kidnapped me? Is he going to come back?" she asked, almost afraid to ask because she didn't really want to hear the answer.

"No," Luke said, his mouth tightening in a sharp line as though trying to keep himself from bursting out in anger. "You will never need to worry about Phillip Heaton again. He'll be going to prison for a very long time, possibly for the rest of his life. My friends will make sure he never gets out."

"Umm...okay." Demi really didn't know what else to say.

His confidence that she'd never need to worry about the man coming back to hurt her was helpful, but it also made her wonder how he and his friends knew he'd never be released. She shared a look with Oliver, who seemed to be just as confused as she was over it, only turning away when the shrug he gave made her want to groan at being jostled even a little.

"Time to go to the hospital," Oliver announced. Apparently, she didn't hide her pain as well as she thought.

A man and woman pushing a gurney came into the clearing, and Oliver gently picked her up before moving toward them.

"I can walk," she insisted, not really putting much effort into her words.

"I know you can," he said, depositing her gently on the gurney, not stepping back as the paramedics went around him to stabilize her.

"Thanks for staying with me."

Oliver leaned down and gave her a soft kiss before they started down the driveway to the ambulance waiting for them.

42

After the ride to the hospital, Demi was quickly brought to a curtained-off room and checked out. She had to stay for a few hours for observation, but Oliver was happy to hear that other than a black eye and a split lip she had nothing more than some small abrasions from the ropes along her arms and minor bruising. Thankfully, she didn't have a concussion or other head injury, and no broken bones.

She was slightly dehydrated and had some remaining symptoms from the drug they gave Demi to knock her out, both of which were helped with an IV.

When they were done with their examination, Demi's cuts were cleaned and covered before she was moved to a small room to rest.

He stayed with her the whole time, doing no more than stepping out of the way whenever a doctor or nurse came by to check on her. There was no way he was going to let her go through this on her own.

He felt like he had finally found the one person who completed him. And he almost screwed it all up. That would not happen again. He would be there for her so much, she'd probably get sick of him and tell him to go away, he thought with a chuckle. Oliver hoped it would be years before they got to that point.

As he watched her sleep in the hospital bed, Oliver decided he would need to readjust his work schedule again. He wanted to spend as much time with Demi as possible.

From now on, they'd wake up together in the mornings. They'd drive into work together, see each other throughout the day, and then they would come home and relax. Maybe they'd make dinner together, and he would love to have her input on some of his new recipes for the resort.

Oliver's days of working seven days a week were over. They would need some time off together.

Luke had come by to tell him Katia dropped off his car and to give an update on the men who kidnapped Demi. It turned out Phillip Heaton was a bigger deal than they first thought. He had connections to politicians and other high-powered people in the area, with aspirations of his own political career. Yet he was also running a mobster-like business on the side—bribing and blackmailing everyone from politicians to his own employees to the small shop owner on the corner.

The two men arrested with him were his henchmen, hired to carry out any unpleasant tasks, like recovering the items Demi found in her attic and, it turns out, murdering her parents.

Luke also mentioned how lucky Phillip Heaton's receptionist was after an attempt on her life. His contacts were looking closer at the incident and trying to find who else was working for the man. With the men they arrested down in Cypress Bay, Phillip Heaton had to have others to do his dirty work for him.

With all the corruption and crimes committed—including murder and attempted murder—they'd all be locked up for a very long time. Oliver wished Demi could put this all behind her once and for all, but Luke said she would most likely need to testify in each of the trials.

It could have been so much worse, Oliver thought later on as he drove Demi to his house. After hearing everything that Luke knew about the men—and no, Oliver didn't believe he was told everything—there was no way he was going to let her stay at her own house.

The men responsible may have been arrested and no longer an issue for her, but that didn't mean she was out of danger. Besides, he felt they had just found each other again. He couldn't bear being away from her. What if she woke up with nightmares? Or someone else who worked for this Phillip Heaton decided they would pick up where he left off?

No, she wasn't going back to her house. If it were up to him, Demi would move into his house permanently.

Tonight.

Pulling into his driveway, Oliver parked before turning to Demi. She'd passed out from exhaustion almost as soon as he got her buckled into his car. Her head angled oddly in a way he thought would be uncomfortable. He didn't want to wake her up, but he wasn't sure how else to get her into the house. She'd most likely wake up if he tried to carry her in. Best to wake her gently, he decided.

"Demi," he began, stroking his fingers over the side of her face that was not hurt. "Come on, sweetheart, we're home."

She groaned, her eyes fluttering open. "Hey, what are you doing here?" she asked groggily.

He wondered where she thought they were. She was on some meds to help her with the pain, so she was probably still groggy from them. "You're in my car. You just got out of the hospital. Let me come around and I'll help you out."

"'Kay," she muttered, closing her eyes again and falling back to sleep.

Guess he would carry her in after all. Getting out of the car and carefully closing his door to avoid startling her, Oliver walked over to his front door. After getting it unlocked and opened, he turned on the entry light before returning to the car. He opened the passenger door of his car and removed the seatbelt from around Demi, taking a moment to stare at her sleeping.

Her face swollen and bruised, and her eye beginning to blacken around it, had his anger swell again thinking about what she went through. She must have been terrified. One moment she was sitting on her dock, and the next she was tied up with strange men yelling, threatening, and hitting her.

His hands clenched at his sides. If those men were in front of him now, he'd see how they felt being beaten on. But he couldn't let himself feel that anger now. The men who kidnapped her were in jail, and he was here with Demi. He needed to concentrate on taking care of her and vowed she would come first in his life from now on.

Oliver wrapped one arm under her legs just above her knees and the other at her back, carefully pulling her out of the car, making sure he didn't bump her head on the door frame.

Once he had her out, he adjusted her in his arms to make sure he wouldn't drop her. He would never forgive himself if he did. Closing the car door with his hip, he told himself he would come back to lock it after he got Demi inside and settled.

Walking into his home, he kicked his front door closed with his foot—he'd come back to lock that, too—and continued past the kitchen, through the living room, and down the hallway to his master bedroom. Oliver set her down on his comforter and removed her shoes, placing them on the floor next to the bed.

Standing next to the bed looking down at her, he pondered whether to leave her in the clothes she was wearing or not. Katia had brought not only his car to the hospital but a change of clothes for Demi, too. She was wearing a pair of yoga pants and a t-shirt. His cousin said she didn't know what Demi would like, so brought what she thought were the most comfortable clothes she could find. A clean pair of socks and panties were also in the bag she brought, sans bra.

Deciding she should be comfortable enough with what she was wearing, Oliver went over to the other side of the bed and flipped the covers, reaching over the bed and picking up Demi once again to move her to the other side. He flipped the covers back over her, tucking her in.

Maybe if he concentrated on getting everything locked up, checking out the house to make sure it was secure, and then getting ready for bed himself would help to calm him. Every time he looked at what they did to Demi, he felt himself ready to lose it, but he also knew that wouldn't help. He needed to distract himself.

Following through on his tasks, Oliver stepped out of the bathroom and walked over to his bed. He placed her mother's rosary beads retrieved from her dock on the side table next to her before getting under the covers.

Scooting over to Demi, he took her into his arms. She sighed in her sleep, wrapping an arm over his waist, her leg tangled with his own. He helped her carefully place the non-injured side of her face to rest on his chest, while he wrapped his arms around her.

He finally felt at peace, drifting off to sleep.

43

The light speared into the room as Demi first opened her eyes, groaning and quickly shutting them again at the brightness. She wasn't in her own home or bed, nor was she still in the hospital. She vaguely remembered leaving the hospital with Oliver. After that? Nope, no idea what happened.

Keeping her eyes closed, she assessed her surroundings and her body. The bed was soft and smelled like Oliver. Since she had stayed over at his house before, she knew she must be in his bed. She was all right with that. Demi trusted him completely and knew he would have taken care of her all night. Just because he had been taking their relationship from hot to cold recently didn't mean she loved or trusted him any less.

Now that she was aware of where she was, she paid more attention to her body. She was sore all over. Her arms stung from the rope burn. They were covered in gauze bandages, but she vaguely remembered the doctor telling her she would need to remove them later today to let them air out or something like that.

Demi hoped Oliver paid attention to what she needed to do.

She was already on pain meds by that time and a little out of it. She continued to assess the rest of her body.

Ouch, her face really hurt.

Remembering the pain after that man punched her in the face, and then when she hit it again on the ground. Demi gave a full-body shiver and tensed at the memories. If she hadn't been knocked out from the pain meds, she probably would have been tossing and turning all night with nightmares. It was going to be hard enough going back to normal now that she remembered.

She didn't notice the arm around her until that moment. It tightened around her waist, immediately relaxing her.

Oliver.

She was safe.

"Good morning. How are you feeling?" he asked groggily behind her.

"Sore," she replied, trying to open her eyes again, more slowly this time.

"I'll get you some more of your pain meds. I left them in the kitchen after getting you in bed last night," he said, beginning to move.

Demi tightened her hold on his arm to prevent him from moving. She wasn't sure she wanted to take more pain meds this morning, but she knew she didn't want him to move. "Stay. Please."

Oliver relaxed behind her before he scooted closer to her back. She felt enveloped by him and safe. She didn't realize how unsafe she'd been feeling lately until now. They silently relaxed in each other's arms for what felt like forever, but couldn't have been more than five minutes.

"Thank you for driving me home and taking care of me last night," Demi told him softly.

"I wouldn't want to be anywhere else," he replied. His deep voice penetrated the shield she had raised to protect herself from him the last time he stayed away from her. She shivered again, this time in excitement. His arm tightened again around her waist, and she shuffled back more so she felt his entire body up against her own. His breath on the back of her neck and his erection against the small of her back made her wish she were not so sore.

"Maybe I should go back to my house," she said. She really didn't want to go back, but if he was going to pull away again, she definitely didn't want to be in his bed or his house when he did it. Better for her to leave first, then have him pull away.

"No."

"What?" That wasn't what she thought he would say. With the way he had been acting recently, Demi was sure he would realize he was getting too close again and want her to leave. She was just giving him the out so he wouldn't feel bad about her going back to her own house when he thought he had to take care of her.

"I said no. You're not going to your house. And if I had my way, you'd never go back unless it was to pack. I thought I'd lost you. Now that I have you back, I can't let you go. I know I haven't been around much lately. And I know I've been giving you the impression that I don't love you, but I do so much. I've been a bloody eejit, pushing you away when what I really wanted to do was hold you close to me and never let you go.

"Please stay with me. Be in my life as more than a friend and boss. Move in with me. You don't need to sell your house... we can rent it out furnished. I just really want you to be here with me."

Demi didn't want to get too excited at his words. It was what she'd hoped for when they first got together before he pulled away. But she also didn't want to risk throwing away what they might have because she was too scared to go for what she wanted with him.

"For how long?" she cautiously asked.

He moved his arm from around her waist as he moved away from her, a drawer opened and then he was back up against her, his arm appeared around her once more, before she had a chance to react.

But it was what he held in his hand that surprised her the most.

"Forever," he said.

A small velvet box sat open in his palm with a gorgeous ring nestled inside—a single emerald in the center twinkled in the sunlight with smaller mini diamonds around it on the band.

"Put me out of my misery, Demi-Lyn Shaw. Marry me and stay with me forever. I love you so much and can't lose you."

It took her a moment to catch her breath as tears pooled in her eyes. This may be a dream, but she'd grab onto him with both hands just in case it was real. But first she had to make sure he'd be all right with one request.

"I don't think I want children," she blurted out. At one point in her life, when she was much younger, she dreamed of having children. But over time, she realized she only enjoyed them when she was visiting friends with children, then felt nothing but relief when it was time to leave.

"I'm okay with that, Demi. It's you I want. We can get our kid fix with my brother and cousins when they have them, then come home to decompress after...together," he said.

"Then my answer is yes. I'll marry you. I love you too, Oliver. I've loved you forever."

Demi was carefully turned in Oliver's arms, where he gently kissed her, making sure not to let the kiss go too deep and hurt her lip. He placed the ring on her finger and asked, "When can you move in?"

"How does today sound?"

"It sounds just right," he said before reaching over her once again. "I love you," he said, handing Demi her mother's rosary beads.

"I love you, too," she said, clutching them in her hand between them.

EPILOGUE

A couple of weeks later, Noah Kerrigan was hanging out at his friend Sean Cooper's house watching a hockey game with Luke. His brother had just finished telling them about the man who kidnapped Demi, and how he was being charged with embezzlement, murder, kidnapping, attempted murder, and a bunch of other charges.

The man wouldn't be getting out of prison for quite some time. Never, if Luke was correct.

Though it took some time getting there, Demi and Oliver were now living together, and she was resting up after her ordeal. He was happy for them, even if he thought they moved a little fast. Of course, Oliver's brother Simon moved even faster and was already married after only knowing Aylin for a short time.

Still, he was happy for them.

"Why is it our cousins can't have a relationship without their women getting into some sort of trouble first?" Luke asked.

"Who knows? I've stitched up and checked over too many of

our family members already. I hope it doesn't become a pattern," he wryly said.

He had nothing to do with stitching up Demi, but Oliver brought her into the clinic a couple of days ago to have those stitches removed and to make sure her injuries were healing.

"This is becoming the new normal. I wonder which of you two are next?" Sean jokingly said to them. Luke and Noah both responded immediately.

"Hell no!"

"I don't think so."

"Don't even go there, Sean. I have enough to deal with without a woman thinking she can find a way in," Luke protested.

Noah quietly sat while his identical twin brother spoke about how he didn't want a woman in his life. He personally couldn't believe the luck his cousins Simon and Oliver had recently. Not that it was good that Aylin and Demi had to go through what they did, but that they found strong women to share their lives with and love was amazing to him.

He couldn't help but wish he had the same thing.

"Hey, Emma," Sean said as his sister walked into the house, closing the door behind her. "I'm glad you could finally make it to a game."

"I can't always go out with my friends. I need to stay home every once in a while to make sure our house is still in one piece," she teased back. "Hi, Luke and Noah."

"Hey, Emma-girl. Still causing trouble?" Luke said.

"You know it!" she said with a huge smile that lit up the room.

After giving Emma a quick hello, Noah sat and listened to his brother flirt and tease with Sean's sister, pretending he was paying attention to the game.

Sean got up from the recliner and walked into the kitchen. "I'm going to grab some more snacks and beer. Want one, Em?"

"Sure. I'm going to go scrub off this clay and change first. Just leave a beer for me on the counter, Sean. I'll be back in time for the second period and will grab it then," she explained before walking to her room.

Noah moved his eyes to the right to nonchalantly watch her walk away. As she closed her bedroom door and disappeared from his view, he looked back toward the game. Feeling as though he was being watched, Noah turned his head to his left. Luke was staring at him in disbelief.

"What?" Noah asked harshly.

"Careful there, Noah," Luke muttered under his breath so only he could hear.

"I don't know what you're talking about," he grated out through clenched teeth. "Just watch the game."

Noah was relieved his brother had listened to him and turned back to the game before Sean came back from the kitchen. He knew Luke wasn't happy and that he had figured out what was going on, but he couldn't think about that right now.

It was bad enough that he felt as though he had already found the woman for him, but couldn't have her. He had been in love with Emma Cooper for years. Only he didn't know how to manage those feelings. He knew he shouldn't feel what he did for Emma. She was Sean's younger sister, and the best friend of his cousin, Ryleigh. If Sean ever got wind of how he felt, he'd blow. The fight during the first period of the hockey game would be minor compared to what Sean would do to him.

Then the next person Noah would be stitching up would be himself.

But he couldn't help but wonder what life would be like with a woman in it who loved him as much as he loved her. He wondered if he would ever have the chance for happiness with Emma. Or if he had to give up his dream of a life with her.

Mentally sighing, he knew it was probably for the best she wasn't in his life as more than his friend's sister. It wasn't like he had a lot of time. As a doctor splitting his time between working at the hospital in Pine Grove and the clinic in Cypress Bay, Noah was too busy for a girlfriend. Even getting together tonight with Sean and Luke almost didn't happen, but his patient's surgery had been postponed so he could hang out with them.

No, he'd never have Emma in his life the way he wanted her to be. He only hoped he wouldn't need to watch her move on with someone else.

Curious about how the Kerrigans got started in Cypress Bay? Get an exclusive prequel about John and Marinda Kerrigan, the grandparents of The Kerrigan Family by signing up for my newsletter by either clicking above or going to www. andreafinnelly.com.

Thank you for reading Coming Home To You! If you enjoyed it, your recommendations and reviews would be appreciated—they mean so much to indie authors.

Want more? Find out what happens between Noah and Emma when they get a huge surprise in Always Been You:

Noah Kerrigan has loved Emma Cooper for years, but as his best friend's sister, she was always off-limits. One night changes everything, leaving Emma with a secret she's desperate to hide.

As Noah fights to claim the family he never thought he'd have, an obsessed nurse puts Emma in her crosshairs. And when the hurricane hits Cypress Bay, Noah must risk everything to save the woman—and the family—he's always wanted.

Available January 2026: https://andreafinnelly.com/book/always-been-you/

ABOUT THE AUTHOR

Andrea Finnelly writes both contemporary romantic suspense and paranormal fantasy romance—two genres that let her explore everything from small-town danger to otherworldly magic. Her debut series, The Kerrigan Family, follows eight siblings and cousins as they navigate love and the hazards that pursue them.

Originally from New England, she now lives in the South, where hurricanes and heat waves are wearing out their welcome. When Andrea's not writing, she's watching hockey, auto racing, Doctor Who, home improvement, and paranormal shows. She also loves curling up on her couch to read, and scanning homes for sale in a climate that's cooler and without a lot of snow.

For more books and updates:
www.andreafinnelly.com

ALSO BY ANDREA FINNELLY

The Kerrigan Family Series

Founding Hearts: John & Marinda (Exclusive subscriber prequel)

Better With You: Simon & Aylin

Coming Home To You: Oliver & Demi-Lyn

Always Been You: Noah & Emma (January 2026)

It Had To Be You: Luke & Gracie (April 2026)

Hooked On You: Hailee & Joel (July 2026)

Finding Home With You: Marinda & Sean (October 2026)

Falling For You: Ryleigh & Dillon (January 2027)

Then There Was You: Katia & Beck (April 2027)